BLOOD MOON

/ / / /

J.R. RAIN
&
MATTHEW S. COX

SAMANTHA MOON CASE FILES

Moon Bayou

Blood Moon

Dead Moon

Published by
Crop Circle Books
212 Third Crater, Moon

Printed in the United States of America.

ISBN: 9781983322723

Chapter One

I hate cows. Lately, I've been fantasizing about killing them all.

Well, let me back that up a step.

More accurately, I hate the watery half-dead mush of cows' blood. Of course, it's not the cows' fault that some tormented twist of fate decided vampires ought to be real and not merely creatures of fiction. I mean, I can't even really do the *proper* vampire thing. While blood from another person tastes the best and can make me even more powerful, I've sworn off human blood for a good reason—an "I'd rather not destroy the world" type of good reason. See, vampires happen when an ancient practitioner of dark magic, or at least what remains of their soul, jumps in at the moment of a person's death. Human blood makes *them* stronger, too, and might just lead to them gaining power over the host body (that's me) and taking it over completely. Guess what I don't want to have happen? Anyway, when that vampire attacked me during my night jog, I picked up a hitchhiker. And not just *any* hitchhiker—I'm stuck as a living prison for one of history's most evil souls.

You say the sssweetest things, Sssamantha.

Yeah, years ago, I used to have a job I loved as an agent for HUD, but this whole dead thing kinda got in the way. Being deathly allergic to sunlight has a slightly negative effect on my ability to hold down a *day* job. Especially one where slow reflexes and squinting all the time can get people killed. So, I decided to become self-employed as a private investigator. I did manage to come into possession of a magic ring that lets me survive in sunlight, which is *so* much easier to deal with than going through ten gallons of SPF five million sunblock every week.

Listen to me. "Hi, I'm a vampire with a magic ring!" If I wasn't living this, I'd think anyone who said that and meant it ought to get fitted for a straitjacket. But, as bizarre and unbelievable as it is, it's not even the weirdest thing that's happened to me as of late. Not by a long shot.

Speaking of my old job, I'd almost be tempted to try to get it back if not for the risk that I could lose this ring at any time and wind up having to once again paint myself head to toe in sunscreen every morning. Plus, then I'd have to sit in those mind-numbing status meetings again.

Nah. Hell with that.

Besides, my life has gotten *way* too weird for a normal job.

Every now and then, I get a case that goes off the rails. Like this one. Only this case went so far off the rails the train landed in the Pacific Ocean... or more accurately, in the 1800s. It started off with me trying to find a missing college student named Wendy, but led me to another missing-person issue, her friend, Angela Jenkins. And dumbass me decides to try and help that poor lost soul pro bono, 'cause, you know, that's who I am, and sometimes I really, really hate that about me.

Anyway, I walk (more like fly) straight into a voodoo ritual gone wrong. At least, I think it went wrong. How many voodoo rituals intentionally throw an approaching vampire back almost two centuries in time? Honestly, I don't think the priestess doing the ritual even meant to hurl me into the past. She murdered Angela as a sacrifice and *boom—magic shit happened.*

My naked ass landed in a field right around the time of the Civil War. But I'm not in Louisiana anymore. I've gone elsewhere. And not just *anywhere.* Chasing down rumors that there might be someone in this area powerful enough at voodoo to send me home, this modern California girl has recently arrived in Richmond, Virginia, in what I think is about 1862. You know, the absolute *worst* place to be during the Civil War—ground effing zero.

Sucks to be me.

And at the moment, I mean that literally, as I've got my fangs embedded in the neck of a cow. Never in my life did I imagine I'd be anywhere near an animal like this, much less biting into one. Fortunately, animal blood works just fine for keeping me going, even if it does taste like watered-down crap. I used to like the occasional rare steak, but sinking my teeth into *live* beef? My jackass ex-husband, Danny, managed to arrange a deal with one of his former clients to provide a steady supply of animal blood in plastic bags. I'm not used to having to actually use my fangs to feed. In truth, I'd almost forgotten I even had them. I know, right? A vampire who forgets her fangs? Still, they unsettle me.

However, I'm a couple hundred years away from of the invention of plastic bags or reliable refrigeration. Blood doesn't keep long outside of a body so my only option is direct from the tap. Prior to my ride back in time, I hadn't actually put fang-to-flesh since the early days of being an undead. And I avoid human blood at all costs after I learned about the whole Dark Master thing and how my entity, Elizabeth, becomes more powerful if I consume human blood.

Which wouldn't necessarily be a problem if she wasn't like the most evil thing imaginable.

You've been in the heat too long, Sssamantha. Your brain is going in circles.

True. Overbearing August sun makes me feel like I'm seconds away from melting, and that's quite an accomplishment since I lack body heat. I'm sweating because my body thinks it should be sweating. Perhaps on some cellular level, it remembers sweating in such heat. Truth be told, I'm still frighteningly cold to the touch.

Another thing I never imagined I'd ever do is mind-control a bovine. As a vampire, I've got more than a little affinity for affecting the minds of other people. Turns out, it sorta works on cows too, but only enough to leave them dumbfounded and paralyzed in confusion. I can't read their minds to find out what deep, dark cow secrets they're keeping from us, nor can I command them to do anything. Well, I suppose 'stand there and ignore me biting you' is a command.

After taking my fill, I seal the bite wound, hike up this God-awful dress, and march across the meadow away from the pasture. All right, I admit *fresh* cow blood is a ton better than the refrigerated crap I get from the butcher with bits of hair and flesh still floating in it. It's a good thing I'm no longer vulnerable to salmonella or tapeworms. I've probably eaten enough of both to depopulate an entire small country.

You know what sucks more than August sun in Virginia? Randomly coughing up a chunk of pig skin that still has hair attached to it. That's not easy to explain to people. But it's reasonably simple to make mortals forget bizarre things they've witnessed. How else could vampires have maintained the idea that they're mythological for so damn long?

I wonder what weird, frightening things the vampires of antiquity had to make people forget seeing.

Slowly but surely, I think I'm going native. I mean, I get that it's natural to want to fit in, but I'm starting to seriously talk and even think all formal and old-fashioned like these people. It might be the effect of the magic that threw me back in time. I'm even getting used to the all BO, too, and how everybody's shorter than modern people and they all wear such thick, uncomfortable clothes. I'm even tolerating the lack of cell phones, the Internet, and TV. The constant preaching and churchiness is a little annoying, but it's so pervasive it's essentially part of the ambiance. And don't even get me started on my new table manners. But worst of all... I think the magic messed with my head, making me forget where I came from and the people who matter most to me. The case I'd been involved with back in Louisiana feels like a blur in my mind, one of those things that I'm no longer sure if it really happened or I dreamed it. Okay, I'm sure it really happened but my head is so... damn... foggy. The other day when I randomly thought of my kids, it hit me that I *hadn't* been thinking about them much at all.

That scared the shit out of me.

I mean, all the crazy things that have been happening to my family as of late, I can barely tolerate spending more than an hour away from my kids before I worry that something *bizarre* is going to threaten their lives. That I've been toddling around the 1800s with nary a thought of them hit me like a four-horse carriage at a full gallop.

Fortunately, (or unfortunately, as it's left my brain spinning with worry) I've managed to overcome whatever mental block the magical detonation left in my head. Of course, that means I'm now going nuts trying to figure out how the hell to get home to my own time before something bad happens to Tammy or Anthony.

Or to me.

By the way, nobody here says "Civil War." They just call it "the rebellion" and call themselves Rebels or Confederates. The hated Northerners are "the Yankees"—or "Damn Yankees," for short. They're also called the Federals or the Unionists. Technically, as a Californian or "Westerner," I'm also a Unionist, but it doesn't seem to matter to these people. There are plenty of Union sympathizers here, even a fire-breathing abolitionist on the Richmond town council, but there's no talk of jailing anybody, at least none that I've heard. Southerners are hospitable to a fault.

Vampires don't cry much, but I'd had tears in my eyes the day I left New Orleans.

I was going to miss the heck out of the three people I'd come to care about most in this time period: Colonel Bart—Barthelemy Macarty, Deputy Mayor of the city of New Orleans and superintendent of its police department, his daughter, Pelagie Jouelle, or "Lalie," and her new husband, Dr. James Gordon Bell. Not only had the three of them taken me in and treated me like family, but they'd all learned my secret. And therein the problem lay. They'd seen me change into my big flying half-dragon shape, had witnessed the fury of my claws and fangs, and watched me tear out the throat of the vampire who had kidnapped Lalie. I'd seen in their eyes that they'd never be able to fully trust me again—or even look at me in quite the same way. So I'd decided to get out of Dodge. Or, in this case, New Orleans, as soon as I caught wind of a rumor about a possible source of help around Richmond.

And worst of all, leaving Louisiana put more and more distance between me and the only person in this time period I knew for a fact could get me back to my own time: Marie Laveau, a famous voodoo queen. For some reason I still don't understand, she hates my guts and refuses to help me, even though it had been her great-great-great-granddaughter who'd punched my one-way ticket back in time in the first place.

Actually, worst of all is that I've been running around Richmond and the surroundings for a few days now and haven't come up with a single lead. No one knows anything about any voodoo practitioners in the area, and even asking about it caused a few of the local gentry to get some rather sadistic ideas about punishing their slaves for what *might* be going on unnoticed.

Fortunately, I can play with the minds of

mortals.

Still, as much as it settled my conscience to make them forget about torturing those poor people, it didn't get me any closer to returning home to my children.

I wander into a grove of trees abutting the pasture and flop down to sit in the shade. It's gotta be damn hot for me to be feeling this light-headed. If not for the sheer effort it would take to remove without destroying it, I'd fling off this ridiculously cumbersome dress and try to relax. What I wouldn't give for a sports bra and yoga pants right about now. Ugh.

The longer I sit, the more hopelessness invades my thoughts. I've been stranded here for weeks, and now my thoughts are damn sure set on making up for all the time I somehow managed *not* to constantly worry about Tammy and Anthony. Anything could've possibly happened to them since I've been gone. What are they thinking happened to *me*? What's even going on back home right now while I'm stuck here sitting under this tree? Did Mary Lou step in and take them home? Did something else go wrong and put their lives in danger?

"Laveau's just as likely to destroy me as help me." I rake my fingers through my hair in sheer frustration.

It wouldn't take much for me to influence Laveau, especially if I caught her off guard with an ambush. *If* I could find her again… but with my luck, she's got a talisman or something to protect herself. Mortals who know about vampires' existence *and* also happen to be powerful voodoo practitioners aren't going to be walking around unprotected.

Grr.

I seem to be getting nowhere in a hurry. Not like I'm going to grow old or anything, but I can't help but shiver with worry for my kids. Seems not a week can pass without *something* bizarre happening in the Moon household. And for us, bizarre often means deadly.

A spot of cow blood on my left hand catches my eye, so I lick it, then stare at my skin.

I'm thirty-one years old. Or at least, I died at thirty-one. Still, I look closer to twenty-five thanks to vampirism. Or maybe that's a side effect of my particular Dark Master. I have a sneaking suspicion Elizabeth might actually be the soul of Countess Bathory, who had a thing for youth and beauty. Maybe she can't stand being trapped inside an "old maid" of thirty-something and made me look younger.

At the same instant it hits me that I'm going to look like this forever, I wind up laughing out of sheer morbidity. The voodoo ritual sent me to the past. I can simply *wait* and I'll eventually get home. It's not as if I'm going to die of old age. And heck… You know, this time-travel thing might not be a bad thing after all. If I'm going to pass through time naturally again, I might be able to locate my mortal self in the future *before* I'm attacked. Without even having to *convince* myself not to go out jogging that night, I could *command* myself to stay home and stay safe. Heck, I could even *command* my mortal self to go find my alchemist friend years before the attack and seek protection from the 'forces of evil.'

I could go back to being Samantha Moon, federal agent. Danny wouldn't freak out. My kids would still be normal. Holy shit, this might actually be the best thing that ever happened to me!

That is, if I can put up with waiting like 150 years.

Sssamantha, you shouldn't give up. That is a long time to be without your family. Do you really want to be ssseparated from them for that long? There is one close who can help you.

My eyes narrow. The odds of Elizabeth being genuinely helpful are about the same as a politician turning down free money. Either she's messing with me, or my plan to wait a century and a half and stop myself from ever being turned into a vampire could work—and she's scared.

I know you better than you think I do. You will not be able to tolerate such a long absenccce. Anything could happen to them before you return. Anything...

Did I mention time travel makes my head hurt? I bite my knuckle, torn with the worry that I'm not there for my kids and they need me. But at the same time, if I can simply wait things out, does that mean that time isn't actually passing in the future right now? I think it just might be.

That is not my ssspecialty. But I can assure you, Sssamantha, your fate cannot be sssignificantly altered.

I rub the bridge of my nose, barely suppressing the urge to growl. Desperation must be at an all-time high since I'm not doing everything I can to tamp her back down into the mental box I try to keep her in. There's about a ninety-percent chance the best thing for me to do is let time flow and spare my entire family from having to deal with this supernatural rollercoaster from hell. But I can't shake that twenty-percent doubt that I'd wind up doing nothing at all, other than waste a century and a half only to *still* be attacked somewhere else and turned into a vampire. Who knows what could change? The one who turned me might hurt my children or Danny—or my sister, who I later learned, had been a viable target—to get to me if I didn't present myself as such an easy target while out jogging in the middle of the night.

You onccce told me you would walk into the sssun if I made you harm your children. I have done my part. It would be amusssing if they came to harm becaussse of your gamble. The image of Elizabeth trying to laugh makes my skin crawl. *And I know you cannot ssstand to be without them for so many yearsss. Go as I direct, and you shall find a man who will help.*

"Umm, how about no. I already told you I am

not giving you control. Ever."

Her sigh grates across my mind and makes my spine seize up.

Not control, Sssamantha. I will provide a feeling only. A feeling...

Out of nowhere, a weak urge to travel off to the right comes on. It's nothing I can't ignore, even weaker than the lingering doubt that I *must* get home to my children as soon as possible or something truly horrible will happen to them. Every minute I waste here in the past is inviting disaster. My brain tortures me with hopes of what my life might've been like had I not been turned. Danny and I had been so truly in love at one time, before my death broke him. I'm sure that's what happened. He loved me *too* much, and that moment when he finally accepted that I had *died*, it killed him inside. He'd stopped caring about everything but the kids, giving up on his law practice, his health, and even involving himself in managing a sleazy strip club. Got into dark magic, too. At first, he'd hoped to find a 'cure' for me, but whatever forces he tampered with invaded his soul and changed him for the worse.

And well, that cost him his life. I'm as horrified at myself for how little it hurt to lose him as I am that it happened. He'd been such a shit to me, but part of me clings to the thought that hadn't really been Danny. *Danny* stopped existing that night in our hallway, the night he'd finally accepted I had died. He thought that 'some creature' replaced his wife, but I *know* some creature replaced Danny. The man I married would never have tortured me by denying me access to my kids or limiting me to one fifteen-minute phone call a week.

Argh!

Oh, to hell with it. A tiny chance I could actually pull it off and avoid undeath isn't worth the risk of making it worse or simply wasting a century and change. I stand and orient myself toward the direction she's pushing me to go.

You can trussst me, Sssamantha.

"Honestly? No. I can't. But… on this, I think I don't have much choice."

Chapter Two

In my life, I've done some dumb things.

As a little girl, I used to sneak into a big company farm down the road from where I lived to steal vegetables at night. Hey, it wasn't a vandalism-type thing. I wanted food. We were kinda poor, okay? I accidentally tried weed (a brownie edible left on my father's nightstand) when I was around ten. Full disclosure: my dad had a joint permanently grafted on his lower lip. Anyway, the exact effect escapes my memory, but I do recall it being so unpleasant I never tried it again—and I got all sanctimonious on my brothers whenever they did.

Of course, I can't *not* mention the queen mother of dumbshit moves…I went jogging alone in the middle of the night.

But, that's neither here nor there.

Today's dumb move is brought to you by the

letter E—Elizabeth. Though, I suppose I don't *have* to listen to her. She has, however, successfully set up a situation where I can't tell where my fears stop and her manipulation begins. My half-baked idea to just sit on my ass and wait for 1996 to come around again naturally might have an eighty-percent chance of putting my mortal life back on course like none of this ever happened. (*This* being the hell that is my life.) However, I can't shake the doubt that it *might* be more like a two-percent chance and even trying will mess my family up even worse.

So, yeah. I decide to follow Elizabeth's guiding mental nudge and walk in the direction that feels *right* to me. For hours. Across forest, fields, and dale. Or something poetic like that. That is, it *would* be poetic if it wasn't so damned hot.

One thing that's nice about being a vampire—I don't get tired.

You don't ssseriously wish to give this up?

"It's not the power I'm thinking about," I answer, allowing Elizabeth, for now, the space she needs to communicate. But I am keeping my inner eye on her. "It's all the associated craziness that's happening to my family. There's not a thing I wouldn't do if I thought it would spare them. If Anthony could be a normal kid, not some vampire half-breed, and if Tammy wouldn't turn into the world's most psychic melodramatic teen."

If thingsss had not happened as they had, your ssson would be dead. Hisss time had completed for thisss iteration of his sssoul. He had learned all he needed. You interrupted his circle.

I close my eyes, trying to weather the horrible memories of when Anthony had gotten sick and nearly died. The only reason he survived is because I did the most unthinkable thing a mother could possibly ever do: I'd turned him into a vampire. Backed into a corner where I could either do that or lose him forever, I broke down. However, I'd had the alchemical means at hand to immediately restore him to life. But it changed him. He's something more than a simple mortal even though he remains alive. I still don't fully understand what happened other than at the moment I took his life, I broke the connection he had with his guardian angel, so when he came back to life, the universe tried to compensate. I guess it's kind of like the way a blind person gets better hearing and smell.

At least, that's what I chose to believe.

A little more than an hour after nightfall, I wander onto the grounds of a remote country house. A single weak lantern flickers inside on the upstairs floor, so I decide to take a meal of opportunity from one of the three cows out in the yard behind it.

They give me the 'wild eyes' and shift restlessly as I approach the fence. The one I lock stares with stands there like a deer in the headlights of an oncoming truck while the other two beat hooves for the far corner of the yard. Fortunately, there's enough distance that they're not trapped close enough to me to make noise.

"Easy there, girl," I whisper to her. "I'm only

going to take a little. You won't even notice."

Her tongue hangs out as the effect of my mental manipulation grabs hold of the critter's brain. Biting a human on the neck can be intimate or awkward depending on who it is and where I am (although, truth be known, I haven't done much of that). Biting a cow on the neck? That's super awkward, no matter what. I know, I know... I promised myself I would never bite anyone again, but I also never planned on getting stuck back in the 1800s. And technically, well, this is a cow.

I pat the animal on the shoulder as I stand there trying to calm it down for a moment. Despite my situation, it still takes me a bit of doing to work up the nerve to extend my fangs. Ever since I screwed up in that supermarket so many years ago and a little girl freaked out at the sight of me, I've had this mental block about fangs. I try to forget I even have them. They're tangible proof I've become a monster, and in the modern world, they're largely unnecessary. At least for me.

Sure, some vampires are into it for the kink factor. I've heard stories of them biting during sex, even if they're with other vampires, where feeding is pointless. Some actually prey on humans, thinking of mortals the way most people consider pigs or beef cows. Me? I'm purely a bottle baby, so to speak. Alas, I'm not exactly in the modern world at the moment. 'Extenuating circumstances,' as Danny might've said.

Grr. The mere thought of him and all the shit he

put me through sends a shiver of rage down my body. The cows in the distance sense it and press themselves into the fence.

"All right, Bessie," I whisper. "You won't feel a thing."

With that, I arrange myself as best I can and puncture the cow's carotid artery. There's something to be said for a heart the size of a cow's. I don't really need to *suck* from them. It's almost like being in college again and drinking straight from a keg tap.

Right as I'm finishing up and sealing the bite wound, a man's voice breaks the near total silence.

"Lord in Heaven, save me."

I jump and somehow manage not to scream or whip around and stare at him with my fangs out. After retracting them, I perform a graceful (and somewhat ladylike) turn.

"Why good sir, you most certainly startled me," I say.

A dark-skinned man in his later twenties, wearing simple clothes, no shoes, points at me. "You's drinkin' on the blood of a cow. What devilry is this? Witchcraft?"

"Not witchcraft," I say.

Sadly, I missed that train. Who knows how my life would have turned out had I joined Allison's trifecta of witches.

You would have been mortal, Sssamantha. You would have been dead before your life truly began, only to be reborn again and again in a stupid, senseless cycle.

I sigh inwardly. *That's one way to look at it. The only way.*

Meanwhile, my new friend is losing it, and fast. "Witch!" he yells. "Demon!"

Crap. I stare into his eyes. *Calm down.*

He tilts his head a little to the side, arms going slack. I lift a name from his thoughts, Polidore. Wow. Poor guy. Good thing there's no high school for him to suffer through with that moniker. The jackasses I went to school with would've called this guy 'Polly' for sure.

"Much better," I say, and telepathically add, "*You did not see anything unusual. Just a woman walking alone at night.*

"Yes'm," says Polidore. "Muggy night ta be out on yer own, ma'am. Ain't good times we in."

I walk away from the cow—much to her delight—and approach the man. "A little birdie led me here in search of someone who might be knowledgeable in the ways of the loas. A practitioner of the art. Do you know anyone like that?"

Polidore's eyelids flutter.

"The Frenchman be in Richmond," says Polidore. "I do not know his name."

At least he's not lying. His thoughts flick to an older woman here who saw the Frenchman and spoke of him.

"I'd like to speak to Chloe if that's all right," I say, in my best Southern accent.

Polidore nods and walks off. I follow him around the side of the house to the back of the property where two much less grand structures stand about fifteen feet apart. They're roughly the same size, generally house-shaped, and made from unpainted wood. While they don't seem in disrepair, they still look like one good storm would knock them to the ground. He approaches the hut on the right and knocks.

A nervous girl in her later teens answers a few minutes later, her eyes wide with fear. Despite her living conditions, she appears reasonably healthy. Polidore nods back toward me and whispers about Chloe. I sense the young woman's hesitation and imminent dismissal, so I take the liberty of a slight mental prod.

"This way, ma'am," whispers the teen while backing inside.

Polidore makes no move to enter, so I duck under the low-hanging top of the doorway. The inside is equally as plain as the outside, with a single table, three chairs, and six ramshackle beds arranged around the walls. Five women ranging in age from the teen who let me in to an elder who's probably in her sixties live here.

The girl gestures at the oldest one, on her side in bed with her back to the room. "Miss Chloe, there's a lady here, requestin' to see you."

"Oh, is she now?" asks Chloe. With a grunt, the woman rolls away from the wall to lie on her side, and looks up at me. "Who are you?"

I walk a few steps closer with my most disarming smile. "I'm someone who's lost where they aren't supposed to be. And I don't mean your house."

"No, I reckon you're quite far from where you want to be." Chloe sits up and eases her legs over the side of the bed, but doesn't stand.

Great. Am I wearing the future on my sleeve or something? Though, I suppose it's a good sign she can see something, right? Meaning, she's the real deal. "I need to find someone who is skilled in certain magical arts. Someone who would be powerful enough to undo something that happened."

Chloe regards me with a stare for a long moment, part knowing, part searching. The eyes of the other women all fix on me, mostly in a sort of *what's a white lady doing in here* way. They can't possibly know I don't have it in me to think of them as lessers. My world, the world I came from, is so vastly different. Granted, it's still far from perfect, though. The younger women are cautious, waiting for me to bring trouble while the two eldest after Chloe give me a resigned *do whatever you're gonna do* stares.

"There may be a man," says Chloe. "I did not speak to him, but he might speak to you. No promises."

"Who is he?" I ask.

"He is like you." She waves dismissively. "You will find him. In Richmond."

Oh, crap. I hope she doesn't mean vampire. Please tell me there's no way she can just *see* that. And oh hell no, lady. You're not leaving me with some fortune-cookie level cryptic muttering. I barge into her head again. Her thoughts circle around a somewhat foppish-looking man with shoulder-length black hair who looks a bit like a much tidier version of Captain Jack Sparrow with anemia—and tiny round sunglasses. Chloe had passed him on the streets of Richmond in broad daylight a day ago. The way the man had looked at her, almost *through* her, sends a shiver down my spine.

"I got a bad feelin' from that man," says Chloe. "Baron Samedi livin' in dem eyes."

That's gotta be some manner of voodoo reference.

The other women in the room mostly fall silent at the name, although two muffle gasps.

"Great," I say. "Is that a bad sign? Or does it just mean he has enough power to help me?"

Chloe reaches out and takes my hand. Her calloused fingers, rough from many years of hard work, scratch at my tender skin. The instant we make contact, her irises dilate so much that the brown practically disappears. As if the *ack!* factor of staring at two enormous pupils didn't unsettle me enough, she makes this face like she's either fixin' to go full *Exorcist* and start barfing in 360 degrees, or someone's about to pass a kidney stone. Actually, no. Neither of those are as strange as what happens inside her head: her thoughts momentarily close off to me so I can't see what's going on in there. Holy crap! This woman *is* the real deal.

After about forty seconds, she sways from side to side.

"Are you all right?" I ask in a tentative tone.

A glimpse of a rather me-like silhouette walking along a path of glowing blue light flickers into Chloe's thoughts an instant before her eyes go back to normal.

"My goodness," says Chloe in a weak half-whisper. "You really are far from home."

I fidget at my dress. "Yeah. Just a bit."

"Seek the five paths. They shall lead you where you wish to be." Chloe turns away and stretches out on the bed again.

Whoa. This woman saw me walking on a trail made out of blue light. Now she's talking like a cheesy kung-fu movie. Must be on the *good* stuff.

"What five paths?" I ask.

Chloe doesn't react. Not at first. Her dark eyes flick toward me, having returned to normal.

"That is all I have been given," she says evenly, quietly, her voice meant for my ears only. "Samantha Moon."

I blink, startled to hear my name.

"Now leave us be, bloodsucker."

The others watch me with unblinking stares as I let myself out, none of them likely breathing until I've shut the door. Hmm. I really hope this guy isn't a vampire. With the luck I'm having, I half-expect to wind up stuck in some supernatural political mess. Ugh. I can't let anything distract me from getting back to my kids.

'Baron Samedi…' I'm not entirely sure who that is, but he kinda sounds like someone important. Or someone I don't want to piss off. Usually, those two things go together.

Alas, I often have a habit of pissing off those people who are better left un-pissed-off. Sometimes, it's as easy as simply existing. Anyway, I suppose that means I have to find this guy in Richmond. As if on cue, Elizabeth's little prodding sense of direction returns. This sounds like a spectacularly bad idea, but it's not as if I have voodoo priests and priestesses lining up to help pull my wayward vampiric butt back through a time wormhole.

All three cows give me bug-eyed stares as I walk by the yard on my way toward the woods.

I point at them. "No comments from the peanut gallery. I have no patience for udder nonsense."

Ugh. I really have been out in the sun too long, even if it is dark at the moment.

Chapter Three

Talos helps me cover the ground to Richmond pretty fast, though "winging it" forces me to look for a secluded alley.

No sense throwing the locals into a complete panic. Honestly, people back then—well, now—are so stuffy I think they'd be more disturbed at seeing a woman walking around in shorts than a flying half-dragon creature. So I'm certainly not going to let them catch me in the middle of putting my clothes on. Still though, my flight form doesn't have what one would call an 'approachable face.'

I'll try not to take offense, Sam.

You have what's called inner beauty.

I'll have you know, in my world, I am considered quite the looker.

Did you just say 'looker'?

He gives me a mental shrug. *I draw words from your mind, Sam. In effect, you said 'looker.'*

I chuckle and apologize to my giant, flying

friend, over whom I have complete control. He actually says, "No worries," and that gets me chuckling again.

Once safely on the ground, I summon the single flame, see my spunky little self within it, feel the powerful pull towards her/me, and soon find myself standing naked and barefoot in a puddle, a knapsack at my feet. The knapsack had been airlifted by one of Talos' massive talons and contains my essentials.

Honestly, I don't know how the women of this time period coped with these dresses. They're *such* a giant pain in the ass to scramble into in a hurry while hiding behind rain barrels outside at night. Makes me wonder what the vampires of *old* did when they had to fly somewhere. If I ever bump into Dracula again, I'll have to ask.

Quite close to what you are doing now, Sssamantha. Though, they wouldn't have hidden like ratsss.

"What, they just streaked?" I blink at the wall of a house in front of me.

You forget, this country wasss founded by men terrified of the human body. Hissstory wasss far more bawdy than you're allowed to believe.

I'm definitely more unsettled by Elizabeth talking so much than I am at the thought of the vampires of the 1400s shapeshifting in public. And yeah, I guess she's got a point. The U.S. isn't exactly the most open society when it comes to showing skin. Hell, even in the mid-twentieth century—a time still far in the future—there will be actual cops whose only job will be to run around on beaches measuring women's swimsuits with rulers.

But, back to Elizabeth. She's being unusually chatty. Or, I'm being unusually permissive by not stuffing her back in the box. It could be something relating to time travel that's helping her surface, or perhaps it's my desperation talking. Could even be her desperation if she thinks I have a chance of stopping my whole vampiric rebirth. But, she *is* right about one thing: I know I can't tolerate waiting like 150 years to see my children again. Who could I even *be* after that much time? My personality could totally shift, or God forbid, Elizabeth could latch onto my loneliness and maybe push me to that point of 'screw it' and surrendering to her.

She writhes in pleasure at the thought of taking me over.

Stuff it, lady. This body is mine.

I cinch the last of my bootlaces and stand, fluffing out my crinoline and the actual dress over top of it. As long as it took me to strip, fly, and put everything back on again, I should've just walked. I don't think I saved much time.

Unfortunately, it's pretty much the middle of the night, so I'm not going to get much searching done. A woman walking around alone after dark will attract too much attention, and most everyone I'd want to ask about finding the particular man I'm looking for is asleep.

So, I do the only reasonable thing a girl in my

position would: locate the nearest hotel and charm my way into a free room. Once upstairs, I luxuriate in a bath for the next hour. Or two.

Not like I'm going to sleep or anything.

***

My night proved reasonably entertaining, all things considered.

I had a long conversation with a woman named Mary Connor, or at least, her ghost. The poor thing had been murdered in my hotel room going on twenty years ago, and the locals didn't put much effort into investigating since she was "just one of them Irish." It didn't help that she'd worked as a lady of the night either. She'd have been more restless, but the man who killed her wound up dead himself months later—shot after being caught cheating at cards. I'm not entirely sure what causes ghosts to linger around like that, especially since she couldn't ever get justice.

Then again, I've also learned that most ghosts are just fragments of who they really were. Her soul —her true self—was long gone, having gone to heaven or hell or somewhere in between. That she remembered anything after twenty years was pretty amazing. But I knew that her memory would fade, and so would her general shape, until she was nothing more than an amorphous ball of energy flitting about here and there, to be captured as "orbs" on digital cameras a hundred and fifty years from now.

Anyway, having someone to talk to where I could be myself (as in, not have to hold any secrets back) was a *much*-needed release. It's not as if I have to watch what I say around her. Who would she tell? She didn't believe me about being a vampire until I showed her my fangs, but her reaction at that point surprised me even more: curiosity. I suppose I shouldn't be confused at her lack of fear. She doesn't exactly have any blood to be stolen, nor is she susceptible to being murdered *again.* And, since I happened to be the first person she could talk to since becoming a ghost, she had a *lot* to say, even if she was only a fragment of her former self.

Alas, she has no idea who I might be looking for, as she doesn't often leave her room. The only times she does is if one of the hotel staff annoys her. Then, she'll spend a day or two pestering them.

She found the conversation most fascinating when I speak of the future. Though, by the time I got done telling her about smartphones and the Internet, I think she thought me insane. Or maybe I simply grew tired and wound up rambling incoherently at that point since the sun had almost come up.

I awake later that afternoon and enjoy a few more minutes of naked freedom before forcing myself to get dressed in my only outfit (the irritatingly heavy burgundy-hued gown). Being in a hotel, I head downstairs and set about politely interrogating the staff about the man Chloe described. While poking around in their heads, I make sure that the management believes I've paid for two more nights. Naturally the way my luck works, none of them remember seeing anyone fitting the description of the man I'm looking for. I rush out the door, now worried this person could leave Richmond at any moment and I'll miss him. I'm not experiencing any strange feelings of direction from Elizabeth, so I proceed with doing things the old-fashioned way: pounding pavement. Or pounding dirt as the case may be. Not every road here is paved or planked.

For hours, I run around Richmond asking after a 'well-dressed man with small sunglasses.' While I verbally describe him, I prod their memory with the image I lifted from Chloe's thoughts. Brothels, taverns, hotels, shops, and markets go by one after the next with nothing to show for it. Feeling like I'm never going to see my kids again, I draw in a breath to let off a tremendous scream of frustration in the middle of the street, but catch myself.

Emotion won't help me right now. I need to stay focused and not give in to anger and worry. As much as I think that voodoo priestess *didn't* fling me back here on purpose, I still want to do unseemly things to her. It hadn't been personal. It couldn't have been. No way she knew I'd come looking for Angela. Which makes me wonder what the heck she was trying to do with that spell in the first place? I can't say I've ever heard anything about voodoo that has the least bit to do with time travel. Maybe something went wrong or it's like a bad idea to fly too close to a spell in progress… like swimming too soon after eating or something.

Ugh. None of which helps me now.

Hands balled in fists, I storm down the next street, finding myself heading into an area with large houses. As far as I've been able to tell, there's not much of a thriving 'occult' community here. Nowhere near what had been in New Orleans. It doesn't make much sense to me why a man like the one I'm searching for would even visit Richmond.

Of all possible luck, I stumble across a local police officer who responds to my description.

He squints suspiciously at me. "Why would you be asking after him, ma'am?"

"Oh, just a little personal matter, officer." I twirl a bit of hair around my finger and lean in close. He manages a faint, dumb grin before I dive into his thoughts. Okay, impolite of me, but I am sick of being stranded in the 1800s!

This guy remembers a complaint that a well-dressed Northerner or foreigner had been 'disturbing the peace' at the Spotswood Hotel. This particular complaint originated from a rather churchy woman who decided that between the man's admission of believing in 'other gods,' plus the 'look of the Devil in his eye,' she felt the need to summon the police. Fortunately, the man had been merely socializing at the hotel's bar, so little came of it.

"I believe he said he was staying at a hotel… Spotswood or some such thing like that?" I say, trying to fake a Southern accent. "Could you be a dear and tell me where I might find the place?"

He relaxes into a smile. "At the corner of Eighth Street and Tan Road. Hard to miss. Then again, the place has only been there a touch over two years. S'pose it'll take a bit longer ta fix in the memory o' most folks."

"Thank you, officer." I smile and wave while reading his mind for the exact directions… since I have no idea where to go based purely on his street names.

A few minutes later, I approach a stark five-story building covered in windows. It's rectangular and brick-shaped, so plain it looks like a government office building instead of a fancy hotel. Of course, this *is* 1862. Some Confederates lingering near the front chat about the post office in the basement.

Something hits me at random from my days in high school history class long ago… a teacher I had in my sophomore year, Mr. Perry, who spent most of a whole class period talking about Belle Boyd, a Union spy, who stayed at the Spotswood. Apparently, this place hosted quite a few spies during the war. That, of course, gets me wondering if this man I'm after might be some manner of Northern agent.

Nah. He's too distinctive. A spy wouldn't be so flamboyant, right? Or maybe he's doing that on purpose so no one suspects. I slip past the crowd and make my way inside. Despite the plainness (to me) of the exterior, it becomes quite apparent that I haven't dressed the part for this place. Though I'm not rocking the ragamuffin look, a dress that's been my *only* outfit for several days is showing signs of frump compared to everyone around me.

Perhaps due to that legendary Southern hospitality, no one comments directly to me beyond a few overlong stares. I head straight for the desk where a white-haired man in a fancy black suit glances down his nose at me.

"Pardon me. I'm trying to locate a friend of mine." I smile and poke his thoughts with my memory of what my quarry looks like. The name Delacroix echoes in his head. "A Mr. Delacroix?"

"I see." He regards me for a moment, finding me simultaneously attractive and 'too poorly dressed.' He's about to dismiss me when I give him a mental nudge. "Mr. Delacroix went into the hotel bar a while ago, though he did not say anything about expecting company."

"Oh, that's odd." I tap a finger to my chin and stare at him. "I'm sure he's expecting me."

The man's gossamer white mustache twitches. "Miss Moon?"

"That's me."

"Ahh, yes. Now that you mention it, he did ask us to send you his way." The clerk leans forward over the counter and indicates a double door on the left. "Right through there."

"Thank you."

I curtsey at him and hurry for the bar. As soon as I'm no longer looking at him, my overly polite smile melts into a glower of determination. Cigar smoke punches me in the trachea as soon as I go inside. Gah. I forgot about that. Used to be, people could smoke in bars. Ugh. I don't even have to breathe and it's *still* horrible. Squinting at the haze in the air, I make my way deeper into the room while fanning at my face. Men sit at the bar on the right, others occupy small booths or chairs set up by a fireplace. There are maybe a dozen guests enjoying the heat in here. Between the mugginess and the smoke, this has got to qualify as one of the levels out of *Dante's Inferno.*

A lilac-toned hat catches my eye on the far left end of the room by a window. Delacroix's gussied up in a suit of matching light violet with a frilled thing down his chest, lacy cuffs, and a set of tiny, round sunglasses parked on his nose that have no apparent means of staying there. He's even on the pale side. Wow, dude. You look more like a vampire than I do—at least one with tragic fashion sense. The wavy black hair hanging down to his shoulders gives him a too-hip-to-be-hip forty-year-old rock star kinda vibe. In person, he's a little less handsome than what I'd been picturing, so I guess Miss Chloe had taken a few mental liberties. Though I wouldn't call him unattractive, he's no Jack Sparrow.

As soon as I focus my attention on him, my

ears hone in on the conversation he's having with another man seated at his table, who's a few years younger than him and light-haired.

"Of course, Mr. Fischer," says Delacroix, with a faint French accent. "I share your concerns."

"Please. Call me Obediah. Good of you to offer the table."

Delacroix raises a wine glass in toast. "The establishment is rather near its limits, wouldn't you say? Not enough sense in this place." He shifts his head in my direction, and fixes me with a stare that I know all too well.

This guy's no vampire, since I can see his shimmering aura. He's also not a voodoo priest. No, he's an alchemist, or damn close to one. Obviously, he's not my friend from the library, but I can feel the magic in his eyes. No wonder he's been freaking out the locals.

"Of course, of course." Obediah nods eagerly, then takes a healthy slug of whatever brown liquor he's working on. "The war's going to roll through here shortly, and any man with sense ought to be quite well away."

Delacroix keeps staring at me. "How apt a thing to say."

I stroll up to the table. "Good afternoon, gentlemen. Might I join you?"

Obediah stares at me like a teenage boy seeing boobs for the first time on HBO late at night. "The room's rather packed, lass. Mr. Delacroix here was kind enough to share his table with a fellow traveler."

"An interesting and beautiful creature," says Delacroix. "Please, sit."

"Why thank you, kind sir." I snag an empty chair from a nearby table occupied by a portly older man radiating the approachability of a flaming porcupine. Though he glares at me, he says nothing. I'm half tempted to flip the chair around and sit backward on it, but that would draw too much attention here.

"This is quite a pleasant surprise." Obediah grins. "What brings you to Richmond?"

"I've been looking for Mr. Delacroix." I ease myself into the chair and tidy my dress.

"Oh?" Delacroix raises an eyebrow. "Have we met?"

"It is my hope that you will be able to assist me with a matter of importance," I say.

Delacroix sips his wine again. "What is it you wish from a simple businessman from New York? This whole war affair is such a tremendous waste of resources. I don't understand why the Union is bothering to fight. Clearly, the people of the South have made up their minds. One cannot *force* an ideology on others." I sense the mockery in his tone.

"Damn right." Obediah toasts him.

"Care for a drink, my lady?" asks Delacroix.

I absentmindedly rub the ring that lets me eat normal things. "I wouldn't want to impose."

"I insist." His stare narrows ever so slightly.

"All right." I almost blurt out a request for a margarita, but catch myself and say the only thing that comes to mind. "If it's not too much trouble, I'd fancy trying one of those mint juleps."

We engage in meaningless small talk for a while, mostly about both men's plans to evacuate Richmond soon and head north before "things get bad." When a serving girl goes by, Delacroix requests my mint julep. Obediah launches into a rambling discourse about a particular horse he's been trying to sell, one that's brought rather catastrophic luck to all four men who have thus far purchased it. Not one lived longer than a week after taking possession of the horse, and the animal kept finding its way back.

"I think it's cursed," says Obediah.

Delacroix offers a dark smile. "Or more likely, you're attempting to sell a horse during dangerous times."

The girl returns with a pewter cup covered in frost. A sprig of mint leaf pokes up from the ice, strong enough to compete with the smell of sugared bourbon. Okay, this will be interesting. Never had one of these before, but at least it won't affect me at all. I take a sip from the cup, finding it much sweeter and tamer than I expected. Of course, even food I *want* to taste is bland to me now, so maybe that helps pluck the alcohol's fangs, too.

Delacroix glances my way with a note of surprise in his features right about the time a vampire would've been forced to vomit up a drink.

His previous wariness shifts to something more akin to curiosity.

"Speaking of which." Obediah glances at his pocket watch. "I thank you for your gracious companionship for the past hour, but I must be on my way. Perhaps this latest young man will survive purchasing my horse for more than a week."

"I shall drink to his good fortune." Delacroix nods at him. "A pleasure making your acquaintance, sir."

The taller, stockier man manages to get to his feet without disturbing our table *too* much, and strides off across the packed barroom.

"So, Miss Moon…" Delacroix tilts his head at me. "I am quite curious to learn how it is you came to believe I may be of assistance to you."

I take a larger sip of my mint julep. At least I can enjoy *tasting* something other than blood, even if it doesn't do me much good in any nutritional sense… or a getting-shit-faced sense. Once, the idea of vampires being real would've been enough to make me drink myself to oblivion. After that, I never thought anything would shock me that much again; that is, until I was hurled back in time. The question remained: what other surprises await me in the future?

"I've got a particular problem of the magical variety," I say, watching rivulets form in the frosted condensation on my cup, creeping inexorably toward the scarred tabletop. "It is my dearest hope that you can help undo something."

"Undo?"

I nod.

He swirls the remainder of his wine around the base of his glass before tilting it back. "The feeling your presence imparted upon me initially... such things are beyond my power to undo. Vampirism, Miss Moon, is eternal. But perhaps I misread you. Tell me, what sort of magic are you seeking to be rid of?"

"I don't belong here," I whisper. "In the 1800s, I mean. While I'm not absolutely certain, as I'm no practitioner of magic, I believe it was voodoo. I stumbled into a ritual involving a human sacrifice. Actually, I'd gone there on purpose trying to find the young woman who wound up being killed right in front of me. Whether something went wrong, or it had been intentional, I remember a bright flash... and the next thing I knew, I wound up shot back in time."

Both of his eyebrows go up. "And by what means are you certain it was voodoo? Assuming, of course, you haven't merely left the greater ration of your sense behind."

"I'm reasonably certain the priestess who conducted the ritual is the great-great-grand-daughter of Marie Laveau. Oh, and they were all chanting to something named Zonbi. Had a giant snake in a cage, whole bunch of naked people dancing in a circle, too."

"Hmm." He leans closer, gesturing for my hand. "Allow me?"

Whatever. Not like he's going to roofie me or anything. I extend my right arm, palm upturned. He cradles the back of my hand while fishing around inside his jacket. A moment later, he extracts a small, silver bottle. With a deft one-handed motion, he unstoppers it and pours three drops of a dark green liquid into my hand.

The puddle bubbles on contact, as if my hand had the heat of a skillet. Brilliant gold light swims around the edges, popping with various colored sparkles. Delacroix tilts my hand a little to the left, making the puddle creep a few millimeters. The edges go pale brown, the interior lightens from emerald to grass green. Emitting a dull *hiss*, the small puddle abruptly turns jet black with a red glow around the edges. The highlight fades soon after, leaving me holding what appears to be India ink. Before I can even ask what it all meant, the substance wisps off into smoke.

Delacroix shifts his gaze up to my eyes, no other part of his body moving. Fear wafts off him stronger than the cigar smoke in the room. He whispers, "You *are* a vampire."

"I've been accused of worse. Look, I'm not here to harm you, or any persons. My sustenance comes from cows, pigs, whatever I can find."

You are weak, Sssamantha.

I suppress the urge to roll my eyes. "The only thing that's important to me is getting back to my children, who are still in 2015. I may be what you think I am, but before anything, I'm still a mother."

He casts his gaze upon my hand again. "Curious. Most curious. I thought I recognized your aura at first, yet you walk out and about while the sun shines. Though, I see now how you are managing that." He leans in and looks a little closer at my rings. "Alchemy?"

"Of course."

"Looks like the work of... do you mind?"

"Sort of. No touching them."

He nods and gently takes my left hand again. He turns it this way and that, examining each ring, one of which sits on the middle finger and the other the index. He glances at my mint julep. "I assume the opal is for the drink?"

"You assume correct."

"This is the work of Archibald Maximus."

"And you say this why?"

"It is his handiwork. Besides, he is the only one of us interested in working with... well, you know."

"Vampires."

He nods and releases my hand. "He has always been overly fascinated with the, ah, undead. Then again, he predates most of us by many hundreds of years and was integral in The War."

"The War."

"The war—*the secret war*—with the dark masters, of whom his mother..."

"Was one of them," I said. "I know."

"You know the Great Master?"

"Great Master?"

"Master Archibald, of course. He is a Master's

Master."

"A Master's Master?" Wow. I had no idea.

"Yes, Miss Moon."

"And, yeah, I know him. Who do you think gave me the rings?"

He nods, confusion playing out over his face. Finally, he shrugs. "Who am I to question the Master?"

Meanwhile, we have attracted some attention with all the hand touching, and so I send out a rapid shotgun prompt for those around us to mind their own business. A half-dozen men turn back to their drinks and table companions.

That done, I wag my eyebrows at Delacroix and take a deeper sip of the mint julep. "Thank you, by the way. I've never had one of these before. It's tasty."

"Pray tell they have not gone out of style. Two-thousand-fifteen, you say? Surely there must be all manner of wild things where you are used to. Such sights and wonders you could scarcely explain them to me."

"It's sad to say our greatest claim to fame so far is online shopping. Unless you count boy bands." I sigh.

"Boy... bands?" He leans back, combing at a few strands of hair where it drapes over his chest. "Should I ask?"

"No, you shouldn't," I take in some air. "Mr. Delacroix, I need your help to get home before something happens to my children. Our lives are...

crazy to say the least."

"Are they like you?" he asks, a note of alarm in his voice.

"No. They're both very much alive—mortal, that is. And very much in danger."

Delacroix pats his shoulder then drums his fingers at his collarbone as he thinks. "You do not need to worry about imminent harm befalling them, Miss Moon. I am inclined to believe you about what happened. I sense an aura of powerful magic surrounding you of a type I have not before seen. It may be indicative of chronomancy, or time man-ipulation—though that is a field few study due to its extreme difficulty and danger."

"How, exactly, does time travel magic being risky mean my kids are *not* in danger?" I ask, a little louder than intended.

He leans back, shifting nervously in his chair. "Miss Moon. The most potent of the effects on you is still *active*, which tells me that your presence here is able to be dispelled. If something were to break the magic, you would snap back to where you belong as though you had never left."

"As though I never left? So… you mean that I'll appear at the same instant I disappeared from?"

"Essentially." He nods.

Essentially? Wasn't sure I liked the sound of that. Still, it's something. I sit back in my chair and sigh like the weight of a thousand ages has been lifted from my shoulders. My kids aren't missing me. No one back home even knows I'm gone yet. In fact, time *isn't* passing concurrently back at home as it is in the 1860s. If I'm hearing him right, nothing will happen after the moment I left off from until time gets there again. Ugh. Time travel hurts my head. "Okay, I think I understand. It's linear, not concurrent."

Delacroix blinks at me. "You are rather educated for a woman."

"Sweetie," I whisper, "where I come from, things are a *lot* different."

He grins. "It pleases me to hear that. And you are essentially correct. Events proceeding forward from the instant you experienced this magical effect are not happening because the world hasn't gotten there yet."

"All right, but what's to stop me from getting caught in the same magical explosion and landing right back here?" I ask. "Again and again and again. Ad nauseam. Ad insanium."

He raises an eyebrow. "Well, because magic doesn't work that way. It has already been released and affected you and… assuming you are able to dispel it, that particular invocation would be broken despite the temporal reality of its phases. The part which has not yet occurred, the part which had occurred, and the part which you destroyed. The universe tends to figure out how to abide by its own laws."

"Except I don't know the first thing about magic. That's why I'm here… I was kinda hoping you would be able to help me get home."

His posture stiffens. Brief flicks of his fingers rotate the empty wine glass in front of him. "Ordinarily, I would be driven by curiosity. However, due to certain commitments, I am unable to help creatures such as yourself."

"Creatures?" I cock an eyebrow at him.

"Would you prefer forces of darkness?" He offers a wan smile.

"Oh, let me guess. They have Light Warriors back in the 1800s, too?"

Shock pales his cheeks. "You know much, Samantha Moon."

"More than you know. I'm not the usual vampire."

No, Sssamantha. You are weak. You deny your potential.

Oh, blow it out your ass. Be happy you talked me out of waiting around a century and a half. Come to think of it, if I *was* able to stop the attack that turned me and go back to having the perfect family, the next woman she inhabited might not be able to hold her at bay and who knows what kind of cataclysm she'd unleash after rallying the Dark Masters back from the Void. I sigh out my nose without a sound. Fate handed me this responsibility —not that I wanted it—but better the devil you know, or something like that.

"That's a rather interesting story." Delacroix waves his glass at the serving girl. "Your kind are rather known for trickery and manipulation. It would be against what I stand for to aid one such as yourself, regardless of the circumstances, and regardless of the Master's inclination."

I narrow my eyes, debating what I could possibly say to convince this guy to help me.

The serving girl walks over and refills his wine. "Care for another mint julep, ma'am?" she asks.

"Thank you, but I'm afraid I'm far too delicate for so much drink at once. It is lovely, but I'm still working on it."

She nods and hurries off.

He smirks at my use of 'delicate.'

"Do you believe in fate, Mr. Delacroix?" I ask, leaning closer.

"If you're about to ask me if I think I'm destined to help you, I would say no."

I shake my head. "No, I merely wish to inquire as to your opinion of an idle mental wandering of mine."

"All right." He drinks a much larger portion of wine than he'd been taking per sip, eyeing the room as if weighing his odds of surviving more than another few minutes.

"In theory, since you pointed out that my children are unaware of my departure and not in danger, if I were to simply exist in this time and allow the months and years to pass..." I explain my idea of protecting myself that night I went out for a run, thus preventing my ever being made a vampire at all. "Do you think that plan would work, or would the bastard simply attack me another time and place, maybe do worse? Am I fated to contain this great darkness?"

He thinks for a long moment, sipping wine and staring into nowhere. "If you were to prevent the attack, you would most likely *not* have found yourself in the situation to encounter the voodoo priestess who sent you back here in the first place, correct?"

"Yeah. I'd still have my day job."

"Then you would not have been able to go back in time to prevent your attack on that night. I think it would create a paradox. The instant you stopped the attack, you also stopped your ability to go back in time to stop the attack."

"And since I am here now, I obviously never stopped the attack."

"True."

"So the attack must happen, or everything will cease to be."

Delacroix gives me an indecisive shrug. "Something like that. Time prefers to continue as ordained. Were you to change that, certain events would undoubtedly shift to prevent you going back in time. It is better to focus on breaking the magical spell that brought you here, rather than creating paradoxes that reality will be forced to resolve in, perhaps, undesirable ways."

I slump in my chair. He may be full of shit or he may be totally correct. I have no way to know. Still, wasting more than a century for what now sounds like a high chance of being useless is not happening. A note of relief radiates from Elizabeth at the back of my mind. Yeah, yeah. She still thinks she's going to talk me into letting her out and becoming this witchy super-vampire or something. Either way, I know I'm not going to try waiting this thing out.

"Delacroix…" I stare into his eyes. "I think you want to change your mind and help me."

The veins in his forehead swell and his face reddens. A moment later, he calms and smiles. "Well, I suppose it would be rather ungentlemanly of me to leave a lady such as yourself in a state of distress."

"That is most kind of you, sir. How would you go about breaking this spell? Can you do it soon?"

"Alas." He shakes his head. "The magic on you is uniquely powerful. A rare type of darkness that draws its power from the loss of a human life. All the energy of a soul goes into it. I will need more than what I have here in Richmond to break it."

I cringe inside. That priestess didn't simply kill Angela—she *destroyed* her. Much like what's going to happen to me if I ever experience the 'big sleep.' My soul is out of the cycle of creation, thanks to the whole Dark Master invading me thing. I suspect that whatever ghost or part of Angela that would've gone back to be reborn is currently clinging to me as magical energy. "But you *can* do it?"

Delacroix nods. "I believe so, yes." He holds up his left hand, showing off an ornate silver ring with a red opal set at the top. Black lines engraved on it form a pattern that's familiar in a way, but I can't place it. Aztec perhaps? "This, I use as a focusing object. Think of it like a magical scalpel. However, the bigger problem is the amount of power necessary to interfere with what is affecting you. Another human sacrifice would be an obvious choice, but that is not the sort of thing I am inclined to partake in."

Delacroix slips out of my control at that notion, of sacrificing a human being.

"No," I say, forcing my way back into his thoughts. "I most certainly do not wish to harm anyone. Sacrificing is completely out of the question. How else can you find the necessary power to break the magic without requiring death?"

"I have equipment back at my laboratory in New York that should be up to the task. We will need to travel there."

My turn to smile. "Then we shall."

Of course, it's also my turn to grumble and curse a lot in my head. I can't say I've ever been to New York before, so I don't trust myself to picture it well enough to teleport there, especially with a passenger. Taking someone along for that ride is a little trickier than just going myself.

Delacroix reels a bit from my second mental whammy, and a trace of the dazed-loverboy effect comes over him. Ugh. I do so hate that aspect of my supernatural nature. I can't be romantic with a mortal man without turning them into a vapid love slave. And I need this guy to stay mentally comp-etent to send me back home to my own time.

Interestingly, I never had that problem with Danny because after I became a vampire, well, we were rarely, if ever, intimate. I sigh at the thought of Danny. Yes, I should be more upset at his death, but after all the shitty things he did to me and the kids over the years, I just can't find it in me to feel sad about it. The Danny I married died long before his body did.

"Something is bothering you, Miss Moon?" asks Delacroix. "You seem suddenly afflicted by a pall of despair."

"Oh, I'm just homesick." I force thoughts of my ex-husband away. "So, New York. We leave tomorrow? You were wanting to get out of Richmond as soon as possible anyway."

"Capital idea." He taps his wine glass to my mint julep.

We drink to it.

Hmm. I wonder if Mary Lou ever had one of these. I bet she'd like them.

Chapter Four

After lifting the knowledge of how to make a mint julep from the man at the bar (hey, Mary Lou would probably want to try one), I return to the table and escort Delacroix up to his room, pretending to be his lover.

I entertain a little temptation to do more than pretend in that regard, but I don't want to enslave the poor guy. That's one big downside to being what I am. If I get romantic with a mortal, it affects them in a supernatural way that turns them into subservient creatures eager to do whatever nec-essary to please me. Especially since if everything works out for me, I'll go back to being over a hundred years in the future and leave him pining for a woman he couldn't possibly live long enough to even see again.

Well, hang on. He's an alchemist. Maybe he *could* live that long.

Still. Don't want to risk something weird happening. Watch it be my luck he finds me before I meet Danny or even have my kids. Do I really want to risk a one-night stand in 1862 possibly rewriting my whole family life? Argh. Did I mention time travel hurts my head?

Not to mention, I had a boyfriend, even if that boyfriend wouldn't be born for another seventy years. He was alive and well in my heart, and cheating is cheating, even if the hairy ape was decades away from being conceived.

Sssuch a goody-good.

Yeah, well, goody-goods help make the world go round, too. Not all of us can be evil and reckless, and, well, cheaty.

It's not cheating if the wolfman hasn't been born.

A technicality I refuse to acknowledge.

Since I know the inevitable rise of the sun is going to slap me unconscious, I take a good twenty minutes and make sure to mentally program Delacroix to simply sit here and be a good little boy while I'm out cold. Implanting commands in mortal minds is pretty simple, and the odds of it working are rather in the vampire's favor, more so when the command is simpler. 'Sit there and do nothing' is about as simple as can be, so I'm confident he's going to play mannequin after sunrise.

I'm not looking to be mean to him, so I let him have the bed. It's not like my muscles will cramp or anything if I sleep in a chair. I give him the command to sleep deeply for five hours, knowing I needed at least six hours to be able to function at all. He is to awaken and sit at the edge of the bed and wait for me silently. He nodded. Good enough.

At sunrise, I lose a half-dozen hours in a blink as my body obeys its innate need to retreat into a state of rest. Consciousness drags itself from the abyss in no great hurry, and when I realize I'm awake, I'm far from happy about it, like I'd stayed up late on a case and have to go back to HUD after only three hours of sleep. Delacroix is sitting quietly on the side of the bed as commanded with a bewildered expression. He's got the look of someone who's just walked into a room and forgotten why.

Perfect.

"Good morning," I say, or think I say. My voice sounds distant and not quite my own.

"It's nearly noon," he mutters. "I can't quite remember what I intended to do today."

I stand, stretch, then walk over to him. He glances up at me when I put a hand on his shoulder. I look him dead in the eye. "We're going back to New York so you can help me get rid of this spell, remember?"

"Oh, yes. Now I do. How strange of me to have forgotten." He claps his hands on his thighs and stands. "Very well then. Let us be on the way before Richmond succumbs to a hail of cannon fire and screaming."

"A most appealing course of action," I say,

mimicking his flair for exposition. Or trying to.

He raises his eyebrows.

"Too much?" I ask.

"*Un peu*." He smiles.

Right. Dial it back a notch. I need to stop by the commode to get rid of the mint julep, but once that's taken care of, we make our way downstairs and out onto the street. Delacroix travels light, having all his possessions close at hand in a large pack, which he carries over one shoulder. I'm not quite sure where he managed to get an entirely different (and less conspicuous) suit from, since his pack doesn't look large enough to hold two full outfits, nor does it appear even remotely full. Well, if magic can make me tolerate sun, I'm sure it can do stuff with his clothes.

Our attempt to book passage on the next train north hits a snag when the man behind the counter informs me that the seats are all filled. Right as I'm about to sigh, he gives me a weasley smile.

"There are a few openings left, but they are premium seats. The fare is $100."

Delacroix gasps.

Hmm. Guess that's a shitload of cash back then. Or back, well, now. Ugh. I hate time travel. I lean on the counter and smile at the ticket seller as I pick up a scrap of paper.

"Here you are. $200," I say while pressing the blank paper into his hand. "Two tickets please."

Like an automaton, the man arranges our tickets and hands them over.

Delacroix gives me the side eye the whole time but doesn't open his mouth until we walk away from the booth. "You influenced that man."

"Perhaps."

"That's unethical."

I glance at him. "Would you say extorting money for exorbitant train fare from people trying to flee war is ethical?"

"Well, no, but…" He trots to keep up with my purposeful stride.

"I rest my case, then."

"Miss Moon?" asks Delacroix.

"Yes?" I push open a door and walk out onto a platform crowded thick with people, 'nuts to butts' as my dad would say. "Ugh. Is half of Richmond trying to leave?"

"I believe so." Delacroix points back over his shoulder. "That didn't seem terribly difficult for you. The influence part, I mean."

"It wasn't."

"Did you perhaps do something to my mind as well? Is that why I couldn't remember why I had been sitting at the edge of your bed?"

I flash my most innocent smile. "I did," I said, and just as he's about to protest, I suggest he forget the whole line of questioning, and believe he's with me willingly and happily. I'm not here to mess around, not anymore, if I ever did. It is time to go home, even if that means using all my dark gifts to get there. Truth is, I'm not hurting this man. Sure, helping me went against his own moral code of helping the undead, but screw that. I'm not like the others. Not like them at all.

I draw a line, of course. I would never make a person, say, kill someone. Or hurt themselves or any others. But helping me get my butt home in time to catch the season finale of "The Voice," well, that's another matter altogether. And to see my kids, too, yeah, yeah. Of course, they didn't know Mom had gone on the mother of all road trips. Hell, no one did. Hell, if I were to stay stuck here for decades, no one would notice my absence.

Anyway, after an irritating hour-long wait on the platform, we take our seats on a passenger car that verges on being overfull. I must have really goosed Delacroix, because he's been smiling like a fool ever since our little exchange, so I have him tone it down a bit, and he does. Our '$100 tickets' buy us hard wooden seats in a fairly well-appointed section. At least it's nice for the era. It makes flying coach feel like first class, but it's way better than walking—or riding a horse. Or sitting with the commoners, despite my happening to very much be one. Not that a horse would fancy having me near it anyway, judging by the reactions of the cows.

Oh, and this would be such a massive pain in the ass if I had to hide from the sun. There's no Coppertone in this era. The train eventually gets underway with this huff-puffing noise that makes it sound like it's barely able to move so many people at once. Within a few minutes, though, we've gotten up to a decent clip that's probably faster than a person could run. Maybe. It *has* been a while since I had the mere foot speed of a mortal.

For almost two hours, the Virginia countryside rolls by... then we slow down. About sixty miles northwest of Richmond, we get stuck at the Gordonsville Station for several more hours where we wind up having to get off the Virginia Central RR and transfer onto the Orange & Alexandria RR. Things are a giant Charlie Foxtrot—otherwise known as a clusterfuck—because as it turns out, Delacroix and I literally caught the last train to Clarksville. The passengers are mostly Union refugees making a dash for Washington, DC—or Washington City, as everybody calls it in this time —before the actual shooting war breaks out.

Most of the O&A employees have quit, probably heading north to join the Confederate Army. So part of our wait is due to the lack of anybody to, like, actually run the train. Rumors float around the crowd of discontented and worried people saying with both armies amassing in our path, we're not going to be allowed to leave the station at all. According to the waiter-carriers— African American women in long white dresses and straw sombreros who bring trays of food and drink, hoisting them up to our carriage windows—half the conductors and porters have deserted, along with the first engineering crew.

After hours of waiting, the station manager finally arrives with replacement workers he's found among local retired railroad men; amazingly, the steam whistle blows, and we chug out of the little white frame station at about ten o'clock at night with a big white bedsheet flying from the smokestack as a flag of truce. I give Delacroix another mental prod to keep him at my side and loyal, then decide to try sending myself forward in time to skip the boredom.

And by that, I mean sleeping.

Between the rattling of the train, the hard wooden seats, and the embarrassingly loud grumbling of my tummy, I can't fall asleep. No real surprise there for a creature of the night. Plus the press of sweaty bodies around us keeps reminding me how much blood is oh-so-close by for easy taking.

Alas, I'm on the Moon diet, so human blood's right out. I'm trying to cut down on megalomaniacal evil.

To make matters worse, back in 1862, I'm like a total dude-magnet. You'd think none of the men on my car had ever seen a lady before the way they keep approaching me every time I open my eyes again to "make sure I was comfortable" and offer me pastilles or torpedo bottles of Horsford's Acid Phosphate "to settle your innards for the journey." Nothing says romance like "settling your innards." Men from every time period are idiots, apparently. Naturally, this doesn't exactly make me popular with the other women on the train. Go figure.

Bad as we have it, it's worse for the African American passengers. A contingent of "freemen and freewomen" have left Northern Virginia for hopeful safety in the North. They've been relegated to the windowless and unventilated baggage car at the rear of the train (only about half of the trains I've seen so far have had a caboose; the ones I *did* see were mostly shanties on flatcars) where they made seats out of their luggage. The sweltering night in late July has to be torture to the living. It also doesn't help that the train is creeping along at a pace I could outrun on foot, even in this stupid dress. Worse, we're grinding to a stop every ten minutes or so.

The first I really know of a problem happens about three in the morning sometime after we'd passed through Bristoe Station, after long hours of staring at the ceiling and listening to people bitch and moan about everything from the heat to the slowness to gout. The train diverts off onto a railroad siding and comes to a stop.

Grumbling and murmuring gets louder among the passengers. Well over an hour after we stop moving, a rumpled and exhausted-looking older conductor limps on a cane into our car. "I'm sorry, folks. We've been ordered off the main line by direction of the Army. We're to wait here until they give the all-clear."

Furious passengers mob him in seconds.

A man in a grey suit shakes his head. "What in tarnation is going on now?"

"Why are we stopping—again?" hollers a rotund guy with a giant white mustache.

"Can't you see there are women and children in

distress, fellow?" yells a thin fortyish man with a fancy walking stick, while brandishing it at the conductor. "I say, this is an outrage!"

I nearly add, "What in the Sam Hill is going on?" but someone beats me to it. Yeah, I need to get home. Stat.

Once the furor dies down enough for him to speak, the poor guy raises both hands. "There are troops blocking the line. They told us it was for our own safety—said there was shooting ahead, and they've been using the lines to move reinforcements in from the Manassas Gap."

"Troops? Belonging to which army?" asks the man ahead of me, the one who'd been plying me with carbonated drinks all evening. He's dressed like a natty dude from an old-fashioned musical. Even I heard the rumor that a huge Federal army under General McDowell had left Washington City intending to restore order and rescue us.

"The Army of the Shenandoah," the conductor says, and a groan rises up from the passengers.

Ugh. I hang my head. Great. We've been cut off behind a Confederate army—as opposed to McDowell's Army of Northeastern Virginia only a few miles away.

"So we're in the hands of the rebels after all?" bellows the almost-spherical Monopoly guy with the white 'stache. "The 'Little Napoleon.'"

The lady across the aisle from me faints. Two men rush to her aid and fan her. This seems a bit dramatic to me, considering we've been "in the rebels' hands" pretty much ever since this whole mess had started.

"Where exactly are we?" asks someone else.

"Manassas Junction, ma'am."

I'd forgotten most of what I'd learned in school about American history, but something about Manassas Junction doesn't sound good to me...

On and off for the rest of the night, the puffing and rumbling of other trains go by in the dark, followed by the tramping of thousands of feet somewhere to the northwest. Every now and then, a rattling and jingling that makes me picture the Budweiser wagon erupts in the distance, and just as the sun comes up, a noise like echoing thunder rolls in from the same direction.

Heavy artillery. Followed by a lot more fire-cracker popping sounds. Guns, thousands of them.

Out of the blue, I remember where I'd heard the name Manassas: the first major battle of the Civil War—and I'm stuck right in the middle of it...

My life.

I barely have time to think *shit* before my body picks that moment to shut down for the morning.

Chapter Five

When I come to, I realize we are stranded a short distance outside a Confederate camp called Fort Pickens.

The soldiers had dug up earthworks like river levees on either side of the tracks, mounted with what looked like cannon muzzles, though my sharp vampiric vision tells me they are faking most of them with painted black logs. In one direction, the train depot towers overhead like a giant grain silo in a cluster of grimy buildings. On the other, spread what had been the fields and fruit orchards of a big plantation has been reduced to the muddy military camp of Brigadier General P. G. T. Beauregard, the so-called "Little Napoleon."

Of course, none of this mattered to me since my only goal is to reach New York with Delacroix so I can get my undead ass home. Everyone else on the train has their own places to go. Mine just happens to be in the future.

Anyway, the day passes in a blur of "hurry up and wait" mode, like all those years ago—or technically a hundred and fifty years still far off in the future I guess—when I'd received my Federal Law Enforcement Training in Brunswick, Georgia.

After hours of skull-smashing boredom, the rest of the passengers are as dazed and hungry as I am. No one even asks about lunch. By two o'clock, the sun beating down makes it hot as balls inside the carriage, so no one offers any protest when the conductors evacuate us outside "for our own safety." The roar of battle has grown louder and louder by the minute. Stray musket bullets occasionally whiz by from the direction of the hills surrounding the Bull Run Creek, and several had struck the side of our railroad car. From far away, it sounds like a big football crowd attacking each other with cap pistols and bottle rockets. The famous "rebel yell" echoes out of the distance like the yipping and howling of wolves. The sound reminds me of Kingsley.

I put on my sunglasses against the dazzling glare. And yes, such a thing does exist back then… or back now—damn time travel. Of course, people here call them "shooting glasses." I'd found them in a little French import shop near the harbor in New Orleans. Oval lenses smoked an amber color make me look like Yoko Ono. At least, I think they do, since I'm not on speaking terms with mirrors.

Clouds of gunpowder-grey smoke billow above

the trees, drifting lazily riverward before thickening into a smoggy haze.

"What in the name of the good Lord above is that?" gasps the fainting lady while tugging at my sleeve and pointing up at the sky over the battlefield. An object with the general shape of a light bulb hovers there catching the afternoon sun with a near-blinding glare of glittering silver.

"Why, that's one o' them new-fangled observation balloons, Mrs. McHenry," says the soda-pop drinking gent, who pretty much has the shape of a bottle himself. "I heard President Lincoln was assigning them to all our armies, so we can scout out the enemy from the air. That's why we're going to win this fracas—superior modern technology."

"But won't the rebels just shoot it out of the sky?" asks the woman.

This idea seems to occur to the balloonist, too. No sooner had the question been asked, than the balloon drifts back off to the north and eventually disappears.

"We're witnessing history being made before our very eyes, friends," says another of the men, one who'd earlier told me he worked in sales of ladies' sundries. "Johnny Reb will soon be in full-fledged retreat, and all this secession talk will be settled by sundown. It's just a crying shame we don't have a picnic hamper to watch it with."

Actually, we're witnessing bloodshed—and I can smell it without being able to see it.

Throughout all of this, passenger and livestock

trains continue to pull up to the junction, and butternut-clad troops jump off the cars and rush to the battle. Crews then wait to collect a slow but steady stream of walking wounded arriving from the direction of the camp.

Of course, the scent of all that blood is driving Elizabeth crazy. She's prodding me to go "succor" the wounded. I'm sure she couldn't care less if these men live or die, but she wants to tempt me with human blood. I guess she figures if I'm around it enough I might lose control of myself and chow down.

It's pretty tough when both the devil and the angel on your shoulders are urging you to do the same thing. What am I supposed to do, ignore the limping and bleeding soldiers, some of whom are covered in powder burns and obviously shell-shocked? Hell, most of them are just boys, little older than Tammy and Anthony. How could I not lift a finger to help them?

It's obvious the train is going nowhere while this battle rages—and, by the way, it never did go anywhere, at least not until Federal forces recaptured the train yards many months later. In this case, most of the passengers traveled by coach to Arlington a few days after the battle, where they took ferries across the river to Washington City in exchange for Virginia civilians trapped behind Union lines.

Meanwhile, I'm feeling farther than ever from my goal of New York City. Elizabeth knows me too well for my own good, and after her needling at my motherly instincts, I find myself on autopilot walking over to the encampment, once I give Delacroix a mental prod to stay put.

And it all starts with a single involuntary step toward a wounded young man perched on the ledge of a dusty cattle car.

"Yesss, Sssamantha. You know you're doing the right thing…"

Maybe I already salivated. Or maybe some hunger that burned in my eyes even through my shades spook him, because he trembles and flinches away from me, trying to hide his leg.

"Don't worry, Private—I'm a trained nurse," I say. Okay, that's not strictly speaking true, but I figure anybody who'd completed a modern CPR and first aid course counts basically as a medical expert in the world of 1862. And before I'd left New Orleans, I'd assisted Lalie's husband, Dr. James Bell, numerous times; in fact, I'd been the one to explain to him that infection was caused by the microscopic bacteria he referred to as "animalcules."

"The doc says it's just a flesh wound, ma'am. He sent all us walking wounded over to here so's we can go back to Richmond on the train. He says there's hospitals there'll take us in."

He had a Southern accent so broad and country, I have to work hard to understand him. Just like most wars, it seems, the farm boys serve in the ranks and do most of the dying while the wealthy city types and landowners buy themselves officers' commissions and fancy uniforms.

As he speaks, a scattered line of other boys in butternut hobble up the railroad embankment, some using their muskets for crutches. A few have blood-soaked slings binding wounded arms or shoulders; others have crude bandages wrapped around their heads. Half will likely be dead from gangrene before they ever reach Richmond. I need iodine and plenty of it.

And even though it's almost physically painful to tear myself away from so much sweet-smelling blood (some of it even left a sticky, glistening scarlet trail in the grass, for Chrissake), I realize I could do nothing here without some kind of medical supplies, and they seem to be in rather short supply.

I could, of course, change them all into vampires. Except that an army of the undead would turn the tide of the Civil War, and we can't have that.

"Where is this doctor you were telling me about?" I ask.

"All the ways across the Portici Plantation, ma'am, and then up that hill yonder, called Henry Hill," he says, limping around to point back toward the battle. "Doc's set up a field hospital there with a bunch of white tents. Can't miss it."

He obviously thinks I'm crazy. Even though every woman had to be a nurse at home back then, very few female nurses worked at hospitals, except for nuns. Which I'm obviously not.

I thank him and jam my sunbonnet down firmly before picking up my carpet bag.

"Miss Moon! Miss Moon!" calls the ladies' sundries salesman while hurrying to catch up with me. I'd forgotten his name already. "You mustn't get separated from the rest of us!"

"I'm a nurse," I say firmly, like a real nurse would. Hey, I was trying to get into the role; it's called method acting. "It's my sworn duty to try to help save lives if I can."

On that note, I march off down the hill and across the cow pasture as steadily as I can, considering the slippery mud, the sweltering sun, and this cumbersome-as-hell dress. Another train pulls in, disgorging cheering Confederate soldiers who come streaming down the embankment from the railroad yard on either side. Officers blowing whistles muster them into ranks below me on the open parade grounds of the Portici Plantation, and they move off toward the battle in ragged columns, followed by quartermaster wagons and gun caissons. As I pass through the camp's tent city, I gaze out over improvised fencing where the many drovers' herds of mules and horses are corralled.

Wow, what a stink.

But it doesn't hold a candle to the stench from the men's latrine pits. Halfway across the camp, the acrid ammonia fumes rise up and hit me so hard I almost double over and hurl. Good thing I don't breathe or I would've fainted.

I hurry on past that over to where big white

canvas tents overflow with wounded and dying—their howls and prayers carrying all the way up the hill, as does the smell of their emptied bowels—and, of course, their blood.

That is what we are here for, isn't it, Samantha? whispers the voice of Elizabeth from inside my mind. *Blooood...*

I set my jaw. No. That's not at all why I'm walking over to the wounded tent.

From where I stand, the rumbling in the earth and the crack of musket fire is so loud I feel like I'm in the midst of the battle, but I can't see any of it due to a thick expanse of trees.

Off to my left, nearly at the top of the rise that must have been "Henry Hill," I catch glimpses of a distant brick house; near me, three white canvas tents sit out in a row, a main tent flanked by two smaller ones adjacent to a small stream. The Red Cross hasn't been invented yet, I guess, because all the entrances bear draped garlands of green pine or spruce boughs that look like the brocade pulls of a theater curtain, culminating in a big round wreath at the apex. I guess so they won't get fired on by enemy cannon. Or maybe Christmas had come early.

The place looks like a slaughterhouse.

In front of the tents, moaning soldiers lay on rows of cots just outside; groups of others sit or lay in the shade wherever they can find any. Inside, as far as I can tell, pandemonium reigns. Doctors (or "brigade surgeons" as they called them back then) work busily sawing the limbs off their screaming patients, their white-gloved arms stained a gory red up to their pits. I take off my sunglasses and bonnet and hover in the entrance for a moment, letting my eyes adjust to the dimmer lighting.

One of the surgeons, an older bearded man with a round, red face, notices me and glares. "By Christ, I'll not have a woman in my tent!" he roars above the din of the screaming and the constant cannonading from the battlefield nearby. "Orderly —escort her off the premises at once!"

One of the male nurses approaches me, shamefaced. He's wearing a slouch cap and loose-fitting dun uniform like a prison convict. Like almost every single one of the orderlies, porters, teamsters, and drovers in the Confederate camp, he's black. African Americans do all the heavy lifting in the Rebel army—and plenty of the dying when they came under fire. They just aren't allowed to pick up a gun and fire back. At least, officially.

I fix the doctor with a hard stare that makes the male nurse sidestep. Despite it being normal for the time period, I'm not about to put up with his sexist BS. "Are you actually a doctor or did you just find a white coat lying on a fence somewhere? You're not doing that right." I point to the bandage he's wrapped around one of the wounded soldiers, a beardless boy with a shattered arm. "You need to pull it tighter to stop the bleeding. Here, let me show you. But first, this wound needs cleaning." Ignoring both men, I move in and tend to the wound. It's damn hard to concentrate with all this blood filling my senses, but staring at the face of a boy not much older than Anthony keeps me focused.

"What's your name?" I ask the wounded kid, trying to keep him conscious.

"George," he mutters. "George Clarke."

I wipe at a nasty wound in his lower abdomen. Ugh. The sight of it makes my heart sink into my gut. There's almost no chance this poor kid's going to survive without modern medical technology, but I still try to do what I can. "Do you have any iodine?" I ask the orderly.

The orderly looks fearfully at the red-faced surgeon but hands me a little bottle.

I let the doctor stew for a few seconds more before forcing my influence over his mind right when it looks like he's about to physically throw me out of the tent himself. These poor boys don't deserve to suffer for this idiot's prejudice against women. For good measure, I make sure the other 'doctors' aren't about to give me any crap for having boobs. The air hangs tense for a few seconds as my commands set in, but the hostility wanes.

Meanwhile, young George Clarke convulses in moans.

"For the love of God, stop that yammering, man!" the doctor bellows at George. "Where's that brandy? Here, have another swig." He pours some down the dying boy's throat, then takes a long pull at the bottle himself.

"I'm afraid we're out of bandages, ma'am," the other surgeon says politely from behind. I turn. This doctor is almost as young as the soldier I'd just treated, but had grown a mustache in an attempt to look older. He's actually pretty cute; tall and skinny with a face like that Irish actor, James Nesbitt. "That's why we're having to reuse those we've taken from the dead."

Why are the cute ones always so stupid? I stare at him. "If you're going to do that, they should be sterilized first or you'll be spreading disease and infection."

"'Sterilized'?" the doctor asks, baffled.

"Boiling them works," I say. "But vinegar is better."

He blinks at me, then he and the orderly exchange a look. I impress upon them an urge to use only clean rags to tend to the living, and they both nod. With the desire, I impart a rudimentary knowledge of disease and infection, and they nod again. Why not? Maybe this knowledge alone will help change the course of the war, but I doubt it. Most of these wounds are too serious for these young men to enter back into battle.

And if they are meant to die, they will die, whether now or later. I suspect the Universe has a way of correcting itself, even if I do help extend a life or three.

"We're short of carbolic and chloride, too," adds the young doctor. "As well as chloroform. Most of our supplies were used up in the first hour of operations. We weren't prepared for all this…"

"War?" I ask.

"This carnage, I was going to say. I'm Dr. Hunter Holmes McGuire, Brigade Surgeon, Army of the Shenandoah." He extends his bloodstained hand, then quickly retracts it. "May I ask where you qualified in the practice of medicine, Miss…?"

"Samantha Moon," I say. "At, umm, St. Jude's Hospital. In Fullerton, California."

Well, I was born there, anyway, if that counts as "qualified."

"Never heard of it. However, you're obviously quite comfortable in an operating theater, ma'am, though I must say you're looking a touch pale at the moment. Do you need to sit down?"

"No, I'm fine, thanks. This is normal for me." I offer a faint smile. "The sight of blood doesn't bother me at all." I nearly say 'quite the opposite,' but restrain myself.

Soon after we get George as tended as possible, another teenage boy in a Confederate uniform rushes in and whisks Dr. McGuire away to saw off a foot, leaving me to figure out a way to come up with more bandages. I manage to pry away an orderly named Hiram, and together, we make our way around the camp, stripping the corpses—much to his shock at having to witness a "lady doing such things." Body by body, we tear their underwear and military blouses into strips to use as bandages and compresses.

Hiram is enthusiastic about the job; not only

does it get him away from having to hold patients down during operations, he also goes through the pockets of the dead soldiers and loots them of coins and valuables when he thinks I'm not watching. Not that I care. The dead don't need them. My problem, aside from the swarms of black flies that follow us around like a cloud, is the smell of blood everywhere. It gets under my skin—and awakens the demon I keep bottled up inside me.

"We'll need to wash these in vinegar," I say. "But I need to dilute it. See if you can find me some buckets and fill them with water."

He shoots me a dubious glance. "The only place for water is the crick, ma'am. And they's bullets flying thick and fast down there. Shoo, fly!" He flaps his hand at a black fly angling to land on his cheek.

"Hey, this is what Dr. McGuire wants," I say, staring him straight in the eye. His body gives an electric involuntary shudder, and he backs away from me.

"Yes, ma'am," he mumbles and practically gallops off.

It's a myth that all bleeding stops when the corpus, as the surgeons call it, dies. Blood continues to circulate for some minutes after the heart stops beating, and wounds keep oozing because there is little coagulation yet. For a vampire, the enemy is time; you're in a race to digest before the blood dries or separates into plasma. My hands are already steeped in it from what I'd been doing, and

Elizabeth's bloodlust is pretty strong. I spend a long minute staring at it, like heroin, dripping off my fingertips.

No... I can't. Human blood will only make her stronger, and I can't let her win.

I wipe my hands off on a dead man's uniform and hurry into the camp long enough to grab a tin cup. I dart into a grove of shaded trees where the soldiers have tied up a bunch of cavalry horses. It's a simple matter to mentally stun one so it disregards me biting its neck, though I only use my fangs to open a wound I can mystically close. As soon as the cup fills, I seal the wound and wander back to where I'd been, casually sipping. A few men glance my way, likely thinking I've got water. That makes me hurry on and chug before anyone notices what's in the cup. For extra discretion, I stop by the large bucket in the middle of the camp and ladle water into it once I'm done with the blood, drinking that down to not waste any nourishment—and also to clean it. People finding a bloody cup would stir up trouble.

Somebody loudly clears his throat behind me.

I realize I'm likely the only woman left in a battle zone of fifty thousand men...

Not that I am in any danger of assault, not being what I am, but I still jump at being snuck up on. I quickly wipe my mouth with my sleeve, which probably only makes things worse, but might at least leave the mixture of blood and grime smeared evenly all over my face. Hopefully, that wouldn't look too weird considering the condition most of the wounded soldiers are in.

"I have a fresh stack of bandages for you," I say as I turn around—then freeze at the sight of the man's face. It takes me a moment to register who stands before me. My vision takes in the white medical smock from his neck down to his boots, the fabric steeped in bright red blood; he looks pretty much like me, covered in gore.

Dr. James Bell from New Orleans. Lalie's husband. One of the three beloved people I'd left behind in that town, but had hoped against hope never to have to set eyes on ever again…

"Sam?" he asks in a trembling, astounded voice. A voice with a gentle Scottish burr. "What the—what are you doing here?"

He's about thirty, tall for a man back then, with sandy hair and a pink complexion flushed bright red from the sun. His beard looks unkempt and gingery, but I would have recognized him anywhere.

"I could ask you the same question!" I say. "Why aren't you in New Orleans with Lalie and your"—I almost say "her," because the child wasn't his—"new baby?"

People might think I'd lived in Louisiana a while; I'd pronounced it "Nyawleeuns" like a native.

He hangs his head. "Sickly. The birth was difficult, and she's… changed a bit. You shouldn't have deserted us like that, Sam. We needed you there, particularly the colonel." He takes my hand,

and it's my turn to look away.

I say, "You know why I had to go, James, after what the three of you saw and the way you looked at me afterward. No way of unseeing that after the genie was out of the bottle."

Of course, I could have commanded him to forget... but such lifelong commands rarely stuck, from what I understood. More than likely, it would have worn off, and he would still be standing here now, looking at me the way he did.

"Aye, I understand it well enough... now. I had to get away, too, Sam. Things were too gloomy at home between Lalie and me. So I signed up as Chief Surgeon with Colonel Wheat's regiment, the one he raised in New Orleans with private money. Including the colonel's. The Louisiana Tigers, they're called."

We walk together toward the hospital tents. For now, I've managed to appease, if not sate, my hunger. I can live with appeased.

"And an eviller collection of ruffians you'll never see," he says. "Prison scum and unemployed Irish dockhands, a few former pirates like Wheat himself, the rest of them runaway farm boys and a few Creole gentlemen officers. A lucky thing this battle broke out—General Beauregard already had half the regiment arrested or put on report for thieving and brawling."

"Where are they now?" I ask.

"In retreat all around us, I'm afraid. I suspect the battle is lost. Our position was to the north, across the Bull Run—Wheat took it into his head to make some lunatic charge from there on the Union lines. We were repulsed under withering fire and Wheat was shot through both lungs. It's too bad; he's a remarkably likable fellow for an old filibustier, and the men love him like a father. That's half his blood covering my coat. I was just now operating on him."

A "filibustier" is what the New Orleans French call a pirate or a highwayman.

James gives a sad smile. "I told him before I cut him open that no man had ever survived such a wound. He says, 'Well then, I will put my case on record.' After I finished, I had to take a minute away to smoke my pipe, forgetting I was out of tobacco. Then I saw you."

"I was feeding, James. Horse blood this time."

He had seen me tear out Victor de Boré's throat. In spite of which, the vampire son-of-a-bitch had almost killed me anyway; James had saved me by stabbing de Boré through the heart from behind with a silver bouquet pin. I could never repay that debt.

"I know, Sam. At least you're taking it from horses and not these poor boys. But why are you here?"

"I was making for New York City," I say with a bitter smile. "Guess I was too late—my train was the last one out of Richmond, but we got caught in the troop lines. I've got a chance to get home again, and I have to take it."

He nods. "Aye. Assuming this war doesn't kill you first."

For the first time in a long while, I laugh. "I'm not so worried about that… but…"

I glance over my shoulder back toward where the train sits. Delacroix isn't immortal; meaning, I can't let the Frenchman die.

Chapter Six

The roar of battle only gets louder as we make our way back to the field hospital, passed by a pair of protesting mules pulling lumbering ambulance wagons. A trickle of retreating soldiers comes through the trees from higher up, a few running headlong in panic and even abandoning their muskets and packs.

"We're lost!" some cry.

"Save yourselves!" shouts one voice above the others. "The Yankees is broke through our lines!"

A sergeant carrying a pistol strides up behind us and trips one of the men, whipping at another with a cane. "Back into ranks!" he screams, "or you'll be shot for cowardice! What regiment are you men with?"

Several more run off in the direction of the camp, but the two he'd caught stood still, staring shamefaced at the ground.

"Barney Bee's Virginians, Sarge," one of them mutters. "But the General got himself all shot to pieces and is likely to die. That's him in the ambulance yonder."

"Then you two little pissants better go with him and help the orderlies. You won't do much good back in the firing line with no weapons, will you? But if I ever see either of you running away again, I'll shoot you like the damn dogs you are!"

A volley of cannon fire drowns out the rest of his words, followed by a loud cheer from thousands of voices from over the hill. It takes me a moment to realize that the guns are booming in the other direction.

"I'd better see to General Bee," says James before breaking into a trot after the wagon.

I consider my options and decide to assist a friend. On the way, I pay another visit to the horses, this time drinking my fill without being noticed. By the time I catch up to him, he's organizing a new operating theater in the sunlight in front of the tents.

"I think the lighting will be better out here for the next few hours." He lowers his voice. "Is the sun too bright for you to assist me, Sam?"

I shake my head. Vampires are nocturnal, true, so I'm never at my best during the day, but as long as I have my trinkets, I can still function. I wipe my hands on the only part of my skirt still halfway clean, then put my sunglasses back on. The first clouds of gun smoke drift over the hill from the other side, darkening the day like an eclipse.

"I'll be fine," I say. And for some reason, I know I speak the truth. I'd fed—at last. I felt like I could "lick all them nimrods, lady," as one of the dying soldiers whispered to me earlier. And Elizabeth and her need for human blood be damned.

The rest of the afternoon passes in a blur of deafening booms punctuated by the constant fusillade of gunfire over the screams of the wounded and dying. The trickle of injured to the grove where we set up soon becomes a flood. Most are suffering from diarrhea on top of everything else, so you can guess who winds up stuck with bedpan duty between amputations. Right... the woman. It's a good thing I have experience being a mom, or I would have been useless.

The dying moan or pray, the lightly wounded full of stories of battle, mostly about how when all seemed lost, General Jackson's men had held against the Yankee advance. "Like a stone wall," General Bee called it, seconds before a bullet struck him down, and the name stuck.

"Ol' Stonewall'll chase 'em all the ways back to Washington," says one bugler excitedly as I stitch up where a bayonet had torn half his scalp off. "You'll see, ma'am."

"You need to keep this clean now," I say when I finished, then task him to wave the flies off General Bee, who'd gone unconscious from morphine and the effects of his wound.

James' commander, Roberson Wheat, on the other hand, sat up to play cards with an enlisted man despite being shot through both lungs. Odds are about fifty-fifty they would all be dead of gangrene by end of the week. I shake my head despairingly at the thought. The bugle-boy with the head wound really was a boy, maybe halfway through fifteen.

The day continues to darken, and several of the men talk about Judgment Day descending on us for their sins in killing their brothers. At some point after four o'clock, an overwhelming wave of cheering breaks out, and minutes later, a courier gallops down Henry House Hill shouting that the enemy had been routed. "Yee-haw, we won the day!" he yells as he races by, and from all around us rises the piercing sound of the Rebel yell, even from the dying.

Seeing the appalled expression on my face, James Bell leans closer and whispers, "We've only seen a fraction of the thousands of cases to come, I fear. Samantha, what is needed now is an experienced eye to survey the field as soon as it's safe, and triage the wounded. None of the surgeons can be spared for the duty and the orderlies are not sufficiently trained. Will you take a few stretcher-bearers with you on the ambulance wagons and act as my eyes and ears in this? I know it's a great deal to ask…"

He leaves "of a woman" unspoken, but his eyes say it clear enough. Well, it's a lot to ask of anybody, but I take a deep breath and nod.

"I warn you, I'll bring in Union wounded, too,

James," I say. "And black as well as white. I won't discriminate."

Being a Scot and a great liberal for his time, he shares my beliefs as passionately as I do. James nods and pats my arm. "Understood."

A horse ambles over to the tent carrying a tall, thin, heavily bearded man in a grey general's uniform with a bandaged hand. If he seemed surprised to see me—a woman—there, he didn't show it. "Dr. McGuire around, ma'am?" he asks, removing his campaign hat with his good hand.

"I'll get him."

Dr. McGuire is busy with other patients, but he looks up when I speak his name and recognizes the general as Stonewall Jackson, his commanding officer and, I guess, the hero of the hour. He steps over, wiping his hands with a rag. "General... are you seriously injured?"

"Not a fraction as bad as many here, and I will wait. Merely a bullet striking the middle finger." Jackson had a careful, almost pompous way of speaking, like the self-taught preacher he is. "I'll be over yonder there, awaiting my turn."

He wanders off and sits on the bank of the stream until Dr. McGuire and I finish up the wounded man we're dressing. When we finally make it over to him, he smiles. "The first army surgeon I came across had wanted to cut the finger off."

Dr. McGuire cringes.

"I figured you might do a better job," adds the

general.

"I think we can at least try to save it for you, sir," says Dr. McGuire.

We splint the finger with plaster and linen, and I advise him to keep it soaking in cold water as long as possible to prevent swelling. Meanwhile, my ambulance crew has gotten ready to go. So, I leave the injured to the doctors and head off to hunt around the battlefield for men in need of help.

All the horse and foot traffic has turned the cart track into a muddy quagmire, and we spend more time pushing than riding. As we crest the hill, the trees thin out, many reduced to stumps by the bombardment. The ruins of the big brick farmhouse smolders to our left. I feel like I'm riding straight into Armageddon.

I'm really here. A thought I have perhaps for the thousandth time. *The Civil friggin' War.*

A black pall of clouds hangs low over the battlefield; here and there, shafts of sunlight break through to glint on bayonets and bright blood staining the green grass. In the distance, the Stars and Bars chase the Stars and Stripes, two brother flags so alike I can barely tell them apart. God only knows how the soldiers do.

A brightly dressed rabble of several hundred wives, day-trippers, and journalists who'd come by carriage from Washington with picnic lunches to watch the battle had scattered in a panic when the fighting grew too intense. They'd dashed off in the direction of the river.

The rest of Beauregard's army stays where they are or drops to the ground in sheer exhaustion. Many had been fighting for twelve hours in the heat with no food and little water. Bull Run Creek is too stirred up with muck and corpses to be sanitary, yet men from both sides crawl there to drink from it. Tattered splashes of butternut and Union blue litter the muddy ground everywhere I look. There has to be over a thousand dead I can count from this vantage point. Who knows how many more lay in hollows and behind fences and hedges in the miles of fields and meadows around us? And how many aren't yet dead but are only wounded and can still be saved?

I grind my teeth in frustration. And all I have to save them with are my two wagons and a half-dozen ambulance men.

In the time it takes us to arrive at Jackson's lines, however, about twenty other wagons join us, mostly cannon caissons and the quartermaster corps delivering what food they had to "the boys." Which is precious little, it turns out. Occasionally, a bullet still whizzes by, shot by God knows who, and everybody ducks instinctively as if from rain. Or a rain of fire and brimstone. Jackson's and Wade Hampton's soldiers, however, who have been fighting all day, ignore them like mosquitoes.

I reach Ground Zero with my little army and walk into an argument between soldiers.

"We should be supporting Jubal and Beauty Stuart!" one shouts in a loud but sullen voice. "We could be supping in the White House by morning!"

"Dunno about you boys, but I'm too plum pooped to move," says another.

"Little Napoleon ain't having none of it, anyways," says a third. "Just what's the point of us fightin' and dyin' all day to win us a few acres of farmland? We could be winnin' the damn war! Beggin' your pardon, ma'am," he adds hastily upon catching sight of me.

All the men around him shut up. I swear, I'll never understand 1862. Except for a few occasions, I feel as safe as a Sunday church meeting most of the time—even in the middle of a conquering army of filthy, blood-crazed men who hadn't seen a woman or a hot meal in days. There is a price to pay for all this tongue-tied politeness, though, and that comes in the form of a fire-breathing captain who shows up to demand what a woman is doing here.

"The Lord's work, sir," says someone else, who I guess must have technically outranked him, because the fire-breather slams his saber scabbard against his thigh and marches off angrily. The man who spoke up tips his hat to me—another old-fashioned habit I'm getting pretty addicted to—and says apologetically, "Sergeant-Major Barfoot, Quartermaster Corps. I'm afraid I can't take your orders, ma'am, since I'm in charge of evacuating the wounded here. But I can sure as shootin' take your suggestions."

The first raindrop strikes my head. Overhead, the mass of roiling gun-smoke had hidden the sky's increasing gloom. Remarkably, it had turned a thunderous black, as if the heavens themselves would weep at the carnage below.

"Let's get these wounded men somewhere out of the rain, Sergeant-Major," I say.

General Beauregard's headquarters had been set up a short distance away in a farmhouse owned by a local man named Wilmer Maclean.

The house suffered cannon fire, reducing it to a collapsing ruin, but the big barn nearby remains intact, the perfect place for me to escort the wagons full of wounded we'd helped off the battlefield. I had to do more than a little mental tinkering to silence protests at assisting Union wounded and blacks, but dammit, I'm not going to let them die if I can help it.

After we get everyone unloaded, and I've made sure to 'program' everyone with any command authority to see to it that the enemy is treated humanely, I resume helping out with surgery and bandaging.

By the time the rest of the field hospital staff shows up with their "convalescents," a full-blown storm rages outside with blinding bolts of lightning, hail, and wind gusts so strong they blow over half the tents in camp. This doesn't make our job any easier, especially because with nearly a thousand stretcher cases, the barn doesn't have enough room inside for the ambulatory wounded. And let's face it, barns leak—and the assorted animal dung underfoot doesn't exactly make for the most sanitary post-op conditions. When I say this is a shitty place for a hospital, I'm being literal.

And for "operate," that means "amputation" about half the time. As the night goes on, the surgeons are more and more exhausted and make more and more mistakes. Working from dim lamplight doesn't help either. I'm standing in a scene out of a cheap horror movie. The only thing missing is the Confederate dead getting back up as zombies or werewolves.

"I fear I can do no more for them," James says to me a few hours later. He looks gaunt. Sweat and blood bathes his face. He's so exhausted that he's slumped down onto a feed barrel. He'd saved a few swallows from a wine bottle someone had rescued from the ruined house, and drinks it down in a single gulp, his eyes glazing over. "The president is here," he mutters.

"What? You mean Lincoln?"

He hushes me. "President Davis," he hisses, keeping his voice low. "Jefferson Davis. You re-member meeting him in New Orleans when he was a senator. At Pelagie's and my wedding reception— in the St. Charles Hotel ballroom?"

"Oh, right."

"He'd rushed up from Richmond on a chartered train, then came riding up to our tents. The man looks in poor health to me, pale and trembling, perhaps because he thought we'd lost the battle. He stood up tall in his stirrups and began haranguing the wounded to follow him back into battle.

Stonewall Jackson, who is deaf in one ear, didn't know who Davis was. When I told him, he said, 'We have them whipped—they ran like dogs. Give me ten thousand men, Mr. President, and I will take Washington City tomorrow.'"

"That won't happen," I say.

"You speak like you know this somehow, Samantha."

Half the men in the barn are dying, moaning, weeping, softly crying out for their mothers and to Jesus. Some won't even last the night let alone a few hours. And what had they given up their lives for? A cause I know to be doomed in spite of the elation of the survivors over the day's victory. But, hey, what can I say? Nobody would believe me if I tell them the truth, so why bother? So, I say nothing.

True, James already knows I'm a vampire, but now isn't the time to tell him I'm also from the future. Then again, he *had* seen me transform into a monstrous flying creature with fangs and claws—so maybe he also assumed I had other magic powers, because he mutters, "And yet, I find I believe you" before he falls asleep sitting straight up.

The rain still pounds on the barn's leaky roof. One of my self-appointed jobs is to go around emptying the buckets and washtubs of rainwater. Buckets of blood, too. The floor of the barn, so big that at least a hundred unwounded Union prisoners had been herded into some of the larger livestock stalls as a makeshift jail, was basically just hard clay and hay pressed underfoot. So when the surgeons amputated, orderlies had to hold pails underneath to catch the flow. I carry them outside into the night to empty into the flooded ditches. It's tempting to drink, but I can't let Elizabeth win. Just my luck I get turned into a vampire and I can't enjoy it.

It doesn't have to be thisss way, Sssamantha.

Sure it does, I think. *I've got a big problem with that whole 'destroy the world' business you're fixated on.*

Once I've got the blood dumped, much to her dismay, I decide to play angel of mercy in another way. I saunter over to the two Confederate soldiers guarding the jail.

"Can't let you in there, ma'am. Union prisoners," says the one on the left, a huge guy with a ruddy complexion and ginger beard.

I stare deep into his eyes and relieve him of his saber. "There are no Union prisoners. They all died. Why don't you go get some food and sleep? You look exhausted."

He blinks at me once and walks off muttering about food. The other man opens his mouth to object, but I zap him with the same mental command. Once he's out of sight, I grab the padlock securing the barn door and snap it off, then toss it aside into the grass with a soft thump.

After looking around to make sure no one has eyes on me, I ease the door open and poke my head in. Three dozen or more Union soldiers sit around, some bound with ropes. All look up at me with a mixture of apprehension, hostility, and resignation. I slip in, approach a handsome officer in his early twenties, and slice his bindings with the saber.

"The way is clear straight from here to the water. Take your men and go, follow the creek north." I hand him the sword. "Be quick."

The mood in the room shifts in an instant to silent elation. Leaving the man to cut his men free, I duck out of the barn and make my way back over to the camp. While I might be altering the course of the future, I can't let them rot in there.

Chapter Seven

Right. Now that I've done as much as I believe I possibly can for the wounded and even the Union prisoners, I hurry back over to the train area where the passengers have all gone back inside the cars to get out of the storm.

My worst fears are realized when I return to my seat and find Delacroix missing.

Shit.

I rush to the end of the car, searching seat by seat, and continue from one car to the next. By the time I make it to the boxcars full of African Americans, it's clear that Delacroix has vanished. Grr! Emotion wells up inside me, a storm every bit as powerful as the one raging overhead. Grief, anger, hopelessness, and frustration collide in a burst of fury that puts my fist through the train car wall.

Fortunately, everyone near enough to have

witnessed that had been more or less asleep. A few sit up at the loud *bang*, but evidently dismiss it as a gunshot or something. I block the hole with my body until no one's looking, then hurry off, grumbling to myself.

Oh, sure, I had to get all sappy and sentimental and worry about the wounded instead of keeping myself focused on my needs. I shouldn't be here at all. These soldiers would've suffered the same without me here. Most are still likely to die despite my effort, and now I've gone and lost Delacroix for my futile efforts.

Once outside, I start searching around for other passengers. Maybe some hadn't gone back on the train. A few shelter in the trees under an open-walled structure full of spare railroad ties. No sign of Delacroix among them.

A stray shot wings me in the left shoulder.

On top of my current mood, the flash of pain fills me with the urge to break a musket over someone's head for that. I storm into the forest heading in the direction the shot came from. Not far from the railroad crossing, three Union soldiers have cornered a young Confederate who can't be much older than fourteen. The boy's left leg is bleeding and bandaged, and he doesn't appear to be armed, yet the men surround him with bayonets, jabbing at him and laughing as he cringes back.

I'll give the boy credit, although he's crying, he doesn't beg for his life.

"Hey," I say, not quite shouting, and rush over.

"Stay back, ma'am," says a thick-bearded soldier. "This ain't no place for a woman."

"It's no place for a young boy either. You should be ashamed of yourselves. He's injured and unarmed. Are you soldiers or common thugs?"

"We don't take kindly to rebel-lovers." The second Union solder, a reedy man barely past eighteen, waves his bayonet at me.

I grab the rifle and yank it out of his grip so fast he barely reacts before it's in my hands. "You three should get out of here before you get captured. Or did you not realize you're *behind* the Confederate line?"

The other two start to aim their weapons at me while the reedy man lunges. He grabs the rifle I'm holding, but I twist it around and club him across the face with the butt, knocking him over.

"His isn't loaded," says the burly, bearded one. "But mine is. Now drop it before I need to fire on a woman."

"Oh, *you're* the one who shot me?" Ignoring the other two guns trained on me, I step and kick the bearded guy in the gut, sending him rolling a few feet. "That's for ruining my dress."

He scrambles to his feet, bringing up his gun too. "You're really pushing—"

I stare at Mr. Beard. "Go away."

My mental compulsion washes over the men. Without another word, they hurry off into the woods, heading north. I toss the useless bayoneted rifle like a spear, sticking it into a tree well out of reach.

"Thankee kindly, missus," says the boy.

"You're hurt," I say, crouching beside him to examine his leg.

"Just a bayonet wound." He fidgets at the crude bandage. "I wasn't even fighting, missus. Jus' a letter carrier. But I have a message for General Jackson."

I help him up. "They tried to kill the messenger."

He peers at me quizzically for a moment, then nods. "Yeah, I guess. Alvie Thorngate, missus."

"Sam."

"That's a boy's name," says Alvie.

I laugh. "Samantha."

"Oh." He grins. "Sorry."

"Come on."

After helping him back to the surgery barn, I resume hunting around for Delacroix. Alas, my search comes up with nothing but more frustration and worry. The thought of being trapped back in time for the next century and change gets me so worked up I come damn close to considering expediting the whole Civil War by killing Jackson and President Davis right here.

Instead, I run around checking with any Confederate soldier who appears to be on guard duty, hoping one of them might've seen Delacroix. An older (and by that I mean past thirty) sergeant by the name of Jeremiah Dolan mentions he'd seen 'some fancy French guy' going with a few other people being transported by horse and cart back to Richmond since the train is indefinitely delayed here.

Great.

Right back to freakin' Richmond, which is like fifty or sixty miles south.

Okay, well, easy fix for that.

At least it's already dark. I head off into the woods until I'm certain there's no possible chance of being spotted. Eyes closed, I picture that secluded alley in Richmond where I landed before, and call to the flame in my mind. A sudden shift in acoustics outside accompanies a change in scenery from trees to buildings.

If not for being stuck housing an ultimate evil, vampire-ness would be pretty cool. This teleportation thing would save tons of money commuting. Since Sergeant Dolan didn't exactly know when the wagon left—he vaguely recalled it heading out early in the afternoon—it's possible they've already reached the city. Then again, I'm not entirely sure how fast a horse-drawn wagon can go, so perhaps they're still on the way.

I head straight back to the Spotswood Hotel. Even at the late hour, the streets are packed with an array of people from children to soldiers to women and even elders. Soldiers and displaced citizens mill about, many desperate faces gazing at me as I go by. All around, voices complain about the influx of soldiers as well as people from the countryside fleeing battle. From the sounds of it, all the hotels are overfull and they've even started invading private homes. The Confederate Army has appropriated many of the actual hotels and turned them into makeshift hospitals. The original hospital is an utter madhouse.

Once I reach the Spotswood, I muscle my way through the crowd and approach the desk clerk.

"I'm sorry, ma'am. We're full up," says the man.

"Not looking for a room. I'm trying to find a guest who's staying here, a Mr. Delacroix?"

He shakes his head. "Not so many *guests* at the moment, ma'am. Mostly injured soldiers. Is this Mr. Delacroix on the list?" He points at a wall, where someone has tacked up two rosters of soldiers' names, one for wounded, one for dead. A group of women gathered nearby occasionally burst into tears and hysterics when they spot a loved one's name on the deceased list.

"No, he was a guest the other day. Has he returned?" I ask.

The clerk examines some papers on the counter, finds nothing, and shrugs at me. "If he has come back here, he would've been turned away as we have no rooms."

Damn! I yell in my head, though manage to keep a calm exterior. "Well, if you see him, please let him know I need to speak with him. It is a matter of utmost importance." While saying that, I implant a compulsion to send word to me discreetly without letting Delacroix know.

"Of course, Miss." The clerk bows.

Grumbling, I start toward the exit, intending to find a place where I can disrobe and take to the skies, but stop short when a young woman rushes up to me.

"Miss Moon?"

"Yes," I say, looking her up and down. She's twenty give or take a year, with straw-blonde hair and hazel eyes. Her face is young, though, and in a portrait without the rest of her body visible, she'd pass for thirteen. By her dress, I assume she works here at the hotel. "I don't believe we've met."

"Elisa Collier, Miss Moon." She curtseys and hands me a small wax-sealed envelope along with a small wooden box. "I heard you asking after Mr. Delacroix. He requested that I wait here and give these to you."

I almost scream 'dammit' in her face, but it's not this poor girl's fault that I missed him. My smile is forced enough that she leans back, worried. I try to relax. "Mr. Delacroix had some rather important matters to assist me with and I am quite keen on finding him. Do you know where he went?"

Elisa shakes her head. "No, miss. He neglected to say. Only asked me to make sure you got these."

I turn the small envelope over in my fingers. The brownish-yellow paper is unmarked, sealed with a glob of wax that looks hastily pressed. The Aztec pattern reminds me of Delacroix's ring.

"Thank you," I say, nodding at Elisa.

She smiles and scurries off, deeper into the

hotel.

What are you playing at, Delacroix? I tap the letter at the box a few times before deciding to find some privacy to read.

Chapter Eight

Minutes later, I locate a quiet alley and disappear into the shadows as deep as I can go. Despite the darkness, my vampiric eyes are quite capable of reading, so I pick the wax away and unfurl what turns out to be a folded bit of paper, not an envelope.

Dear Samantha Moon,

Please accept my deepest sympathies regarding your situation. However, it has been my experience that dealing with vampires seldom ends well for mortals, and those of my particular talents even less so. I prefer to distance myself as much as possible from them regardless of how noble your intentions might be. There is, however, a favor you can do for me. Wait for nightfall one day hence, and deliver the contents of this box to a man named Cumberland. I had intended to deliver the box myself, though the recent commencement of hostilities necessitates my return to the North posthaste. Don't bother to follow, and I mean that in every sense of the word.

Regards,
Jean Delacroix.

I smirk. Not only is he abandoning me (okay, so I was trying to force him to help, but still), he expects me to play messenger girl? Hah!

The second that thought forms in my mind, the ink shifts from black to glowing golden light. Like a string unwinding, the writing spools up from the letter into a thread that floats toward my face. My head fogs for a second and I find myself staring at blank paper.

"What on Earth?" I frown. "Oh. Probably one of those spy-type things… disappearing ink."

I start to toss the box aside, but a pain shoots through my bicep like a bullet.

"Gah!" I grab my arm, shaking from how much that hurt. "Shit!"

The pain fades in a few seconds. Again, I try to discard the box, and the pain hits me again, strong enough to bring tears to my eyes.

Ooh! I scowl. The bastard ensorcelled me.

One last attempt to get rid of the box makes me cry out at a feeling like I'd stuck my whole right arm into a meat grinder. The instant I abandon the urge to drop it, the pain stops. Oh, Delacroix… I'm going to do something unpleasant when I catch up to you. He didn't even tell me where to find this Cumberland person.

Might as well get this over with. Cumberland's not a common name, at least I don't think so. Maybe it is back in the 1800s, though I suspect it might be a slave name since it lacked a "Mr." or a first name. I manage one step with the intent to find him before a wave of agony hits me like I'd body surfed a giant cheese grater naked.

I can't help but shriek and freeze in place.

Oh, you bastard...

I suspect Delacroix thinks he's buying himself enough of a head start to elude me for good, but he doesn't know how fast Talos can move.

My cry attracts two men from the nearby street who come running over.

"Are you all right, ma'am?" asks the taller one.

The other steps past me to look around at the alley.

Grr. "Yes, thank you. I thought I saw a rat or something crawling about."

They chuckle in that patronizing way men tend to do at women afraid of rodents. Not that I care about rats or mice, but it's a convenient excuse for screaming that won't stir up trouble. The men take it upon themselves to "escort me to safety," and leave me at the well-lit frontage of another hotel.

Somewhere in the back of my mind, my mother's voice natters at me that this is what I get for trying to control him... getting controlled back. Though, what he did to me is less *control* and more an unavoidable punishment for disobeying. Even a momentary thought of abandoning Richmond and flying north to New York triggers an onset of blinding pain, so I'm pretty much stuck at least for another day, which infuriates me, but apparently, I've come down with another acute case of magic poisoning.

Once I release all thoughts of following him or leaving town, I find that I can move again.

That accomplished, and with little else to do but waste time, I head to the outskirts of town in search of a cow. After feeding, I return to the city center and *charm* my way into a room at the Spotswood Hotel. Of course, it's already occupied, but the man doesn't mind me there. He can't object to me when he's unaware I exist.

***

As soon as I wake the next afternoon, I head downstairs to the hotel bar and flop at a table, glaring at the little box.

Every time I think to get up and either abandon it to head for New York or deliver it early, the pain starts up. Figuring it would likely remain constant as long as I'm 'disobedient,' I bide my time and daydream about how best to exact my revenge on Delacroix for the indignity.

A strong compulsion to sit around doing nothing comes over me, and I while away the daylight hours in the hotel bar, making idle chitchat with random men who invite themselves to my table. As soon as it gets dark out, another urge drives me to my feet and sends me out the door into the lobby. My body wants to go somewhere specific, though I have no conscious idea where. Fighting it hurts too much, and since I'm sure I can overtake Delacroix as soon as I deal with this nuisance, I roll with it.

I march out of the hotel into the street, wondering where the hell I'm going, and why...

Chapter Nine

Delacroix's damned magical influence leads me to the very outskirts of Richmond.

I approach a plantation house and head around the side to the slave quarters near a line of trees. One of the long huts stands out more than the others, which is probably the effect of the spell pulling me there. Grumbling, I make my way across the field and barge into a room, startling nine adults and a handful of small children. The adults range in age from thirties to a boy about sixteen, the other six appear younger than ten.

Though there's little in the way of privacy here —the interior is set up more like barracks—I get the feeling these people represent several families sharing a dwelling. Some regard me with apprehension, as if they expect to be unfairly punished for a white woman being in their living quarters, but most look at me warily, as if some sixth sense keys them in on the supernatural predator in their midst.

"Is there a Cumberland here?" I ask.

One of the men, a lanky guy in his later twenties, nods. "Yes'm. That'd be me."

"I have something for you." I hold up the box.

Cumberland approaches me with an air of hesitant hope. He takes the box, looks at it, and blinks at me. "Where is Delacroix?"

"On his way to New York, I suspect," I grumble.

"He was supposed to bring this to us days ago," says a woman clutching a two-year-old.

I fidget. Oops. "He got delayed by the war. Guess he should've FedEx-ed it instead."

They all stare at me like I've got three heads.

Cumberland opens the box, eyes the contents, and sighs with relief. "It is here."

"You are putting your faith in nonsense," says the oldest of the women, who appears to be about thirty.

"And what if it works, Phibe?" asks Cumberland. "Are you not willing to risk it?"

The woman scoffs and mutters something incomprehensible.

"What exactly is 'it?'" I ask.

Cumberland removes two bottles from the box and hands one to another man. One by one, the five men drink about a shot glass worth each. Phibe starts to chuckle mockingly at them, but after a minute, her sanctimony comes to a screeching halt as the men go pale. Before my eyes, the African men grow older in seconds, continuing to lighten until five fiftyish white men stand around gawking at each other. Even the boy who looked about sixteen now seems to be pushing sixty.

One of the little boys begins to wail in a panic. His mother scoops him up and shushes him.

"It worked," says Cumberland, his voice no different from what it had been before. "We must leave, *now.*"

"Whoa," I say.

Cumberland, who's taken on the appearance of a crotchety old prospector, complete with a mustache he could sweep a floor with, walks up to me. "I have family up north. They gave money to Mr. Delacroix to assist our escape. This magic will last only a few days. We must leave now."

The men examine each other.

A man who'd been in his thirties before but now appears ready to drop from old age scratches his head. "I understand that. But why are we *old*?"

"So you don't get conscripted into the army," I say, taking the most obvious guess I can think of. "No one will press old men into fighting."

A pretty teen girl stands from her bed, wide-eyed with worry. She's still got marks on her legs from where shackles bit into her flesh. Her English hides under a thick accent. "It's still too dangerous. *You* men might make it to the north, but the rest of us are going to be beaten or killed for trying to escape."

"Calm yourself, Hany," says another man, putting his hand on the girl's shoulder. "Have faith."

She shies away from his touch, scowling at the floor.

I can't help but feel like an ogre for dragging Delacroix away from these people. That girl is only like fifteen. Yeah, the times are totally different, but to my modern sensibilities, she's a child who shouldn't be exposed to this. She's still someone's daughter. And the little ones… and even the adults. How could anyone have ever reconciled slavery with their conscience?

Before Elizabeth can torment me with her memories of conquered villagers being enslaved during her time as a mortal, I stuff her back in the mental box I keep her in.

Cumberland glances at me. "If Delacroix sent you, that means you must have some magic, too. Please, will you help us?" He gestures at the wall. "We are to go to a farmhouse a few days' north where there are people who will hide us."

I nod. Shit, it's the least I can do. "Sure. I will help."

Not like I'm in a rush or anything. I've only got about a hundred and fifty years or so to kill.

Chapter Ten

We head out within minutes, after only the briefest attempt to gather supplies.

Three overseers from the plantation try to question us, but I give them all a desperate compulsion to go help at the local hospital and forget entirely about this place or their duties to the landowner. The former slaves gape at me in awe, and mutter amongst themselves with renewed hope —though Phibe doesn't fully trust me.

Our group consists of: Cumberland and his eighteen-year-old sister, Lucy; Edwin (who is twenty) and his wife, Catherine, two years his senior. The eldest, at thirty-two, is named Ben, and also looks like he's pushing seventy. Grafton, who's midway through his twenties and Hany's brother, walks with a slight limp, an aftereffect of a rather vicious beating he'd suffered for an escape attempt two years ago. Phibe, who's thirty, is Isaac's mother. The sixteen-year-old now looks like a sickly white man in his later fifties, though he still has the overly polite demeanor of a young teen.

The smaller children hover close to the women, and I learn that two of them (not even ten years old yet) are no relation to anyone here, having been purchased only weeks ago, separated from their parents who could be anywhere in Virginia.

Grr.

I don't know if Delacroix's magic contained any compulsion to continue helping these people. Considering I'd only know about it if I resisted, I'm not about to find out. To hell with screwing up the timeline… I'm going to do whatever I can to help these people find a better life.

Near the northern edge of Richmond, a pair of police officers stop us, curious at a group of old men traveling amicably with several 'Negro women and children.' I send them on their way after making them forget having seen us entirely. Again, whispers go through the people with me, marveling at my influence over the minds of men.

A few of the women mutter under their breaths, but the way they're looking at me makes it pretty obvious they regard me as some manner of dangerous witch. Of course, considering what I'm doing for them, there's little actual hostility involved—mostly trepidation. Something tells me they're rather highly superstitious and don't want to do anything to get on my bad side. Voodoo, I know, is highly pervasive in the slave culture. A means to control what otherwise seemed uncontrollable. Had I been a slave, I would have been into voodoo, too. Of that, I knew without a doubt.

I feel bad enough for them already, and having them afraid of me is only making the guilt worse. Still, I don't bother tinkering with their thoughts. The best thing I can do here is escort them to where they need to be as fast as possible and remove myself from their lives.

Soon, we leave Richmond behind and head into the wilderness, doing the best we can to avoid people and/or signs of war. After several hours, the children run out of steam, but Cumberland and Edwin keep pushing them on. Eventually, the women wear out and the men agree to stop for a brief period of rest. A small argument starts about the effects of Delacroix's potion wearing off before they get to the safe house, but I ease their fears by assuring them I should be able to chase away any trouble short of us walking into a large battalion of Confederate soldiers armed with silver bullets. My mind control powers only work on one person at a time after all. At least, that's what I assumed. Who knows? Where there's a will, there's a way, and all that. So far, I haven't had a need to influence more than one person at a time.

Anyway, while they settle down for a few hours' sleep, I pace around the 'camp,' keeping watch. Other than the sounds of insects, the woods are eerily silent. The children are frightened and fidgety, but scared enough of horrible punishment if they're captured that they keep quiet. Thinking about that landowner potentially beating children bloody for escaping pushes me to a near rage. I'm half-tempted to fly back to that plantation and vent on the bastard, but it would be just my luck something happens to these people if I leave.

Fuming, I pace around the darkness. There's so much angst in my head between wanting to go home, missing my kids, being pissed off at people who could keep slaves, and Delacroix slipping away that I can't figure out what to dwell on.

Hours later, a scrap of light catches my eye in the woods. I stop, my mood shifting from a torment of emotion to calm curiosity in an instant. The flickering image of a young Confederate soldier comes walking out of the trees toward me. When he gets within ten paces, he stops and stares at me. In a moment, I recognize him—George Clarke. I knew he would likely die from that stomach wound, but seeing the ghost of a tow-headed sixteen-year-old boy punches me in the gut. All I can picture is my reaction to Anthony dying.

I slump into a crouch, hand over my mouth to keep from sobbing loud enough to wake the escaping slaves.

"Evening, ma'am," says George. "Wanted to thank you for what you tried to do for me, but I didn't make it."

"I…"

"Nothing you could've done." George walks closer. "I'd like to repay your kindness, but I ain't rightly sure what I can do for you like this."

A sad chuckle leaks out of my throat. "I don't suppose you can break a time travel spell, or find a runaway alchemist."

George blinks. "Sorry, miss. A what?"

"I got caught in a runaway magical spell that threw me back in time. Never mind..."

"Oh." George kicks at the dirt, not that the ground reacts to him. "I don't know nothin' about no magic, but I reckon I can find a man for you."

"That would be a big help," I say, smiling. "But I can't leave these people yet. It's all right if you have somewhere to be. No need for you to linger around here on my account."

George bows. "It's fine, ma'am. I can return when you are ready."

Before I can open my mouth, he fades away.

Ugh.

Overcome with sorrow at seeing a boy not much older than Anthony as a ghost, I crumple to the ground and lean against a tree, crying softly into my hands.

Chapter Eleven

The next thing I know, I'm flat on my back staring up at three old white men.

"You all right, missus?" asks one, in Cumberland's voice.

A small boy squatting next to me in little more than a ratty pair of shorts pokes me in the shoulder with a stick. When I roll my head to look up at him, he smiles.

"You's not wakin' up," says the man on the left, Grafton I think.

"I sleep pretty hard." I sit up. "I'm fine. I guess it's a medical issue. Nothing would've woken me any sooner."

"I hope your magic can protect us if the potion falters," says Cumberland.

"Yeah. I'll do everything I can." I stand and dust myself off. "Sorry for causing a delay. Are you ready?"

Phibe walks over to me and offers a wooden cup of water. "The extra rest was needed."

No sense freaking them out. I accept and drink the water. "Thank you."

They gather their meager possessions, and soon we're underway, following the path of the rain-swollen Rappahannock River. Cumberland falls in step beside me, explaining the route he plans to take to a farmhouse where the people are part of the Underground Railroad. He doesn't expect me to stay with them after that point, since he feels they will be protected enough there.

A few hours into our trek, a sudden ripple of gunfire goes off to the right, echoing among the trees. The younger children begin to panic at the shouts of distant men. We divert away from the river, moving into the woods out of sight in case the fighting gets too close.

For the next twenty minutes or so, shooting and screaming continue off to the east, but fortunately, no bullets find us. Once the battle subsides, we pick up our pace and spend the next few hours following the river.

Late in the afternoon, the men decide to stop for a brief rest. Not long after the women head into the woods to relieve themselves, Hany screams.

I rush toward the sounds of a scuffle and stumble onto an infuriating scene. A Confederate soldier holds Hany, the fifteen-year-old, from behind by the arms. Another soldier has his rifle aimed at the other women. I don't need powers of mind reading to figure out what's on their mind. Both of them look like they've recently seen some rough action, their uniforms muddy and torn, splashes of other people's blood dried on their faces and clothes.

Phibe points at the man holding Hany. "Let her go."

"I don't take no orders from no ni—"

"Hey!" I shout.

Both men look my way.

Now, the men come running up behind me.

"Let go of her." I step closer.

"Well, lookit what we got here," says the soldier with the rifle. "Bunch of runaways?"

"These women belong to me," says Ben, who looks the oldest of the 'white men.' "Kindly unhand my property."

"You know what I think?" asks the soldier with the rifle. "I think you stole them."

A quick glance at their minds tells me these two mean to cause trouble. They ran off from the fighting after seeing a bit too much death, and neither much cares about anything at all anymore.

"Alton Chisolm," I say to the man holding Hany. "I'm going to give you two more seconds to let go of that girl before I do more than ask." I shift my gaze to the other. "And you, Fred Pardoe? I'm sure the Confederate Army would love to know where a pair of deserters disappeared off to."

He points his rifle at me. "H-how the hell do you know my name?"

I zip forward, getting past the end of his weapon before he can fire, and slug him in the jaw. He goes down like a sack of wheat. The other man throws Hany aside and pulls a knife, then lunges at me exactly like my old trainer at Quantico used to do. I grab the incoming limb by the wrist and flip him around onto his chest, disarming the blade and chicken-winging his arm up behind his back.

All the escapees gasp.

"You bitch," yells Pardoe, holding his jaw.

"If I apply just a little more pressure, it breaks," I say, with a bit of a twist at his arm. "Give me an excuse."

Chisolm, evidently lacking the intelligence the Creator gave a garden frog, staggers to his feet and lumbers at me. I spring upright off Pardoe and catch him in a judo takedown, sweeping his leg while shoving at his upper body. He lands flat on his back hard enough to take the wind straight out of his lungs. With the two soldiers stunned and wheezing, I collect their rifles and toss them to Cumberland and Ben, then relieve the soldiers of their extra cartridges as well as knives.

"Now… you two get the hell out of here while you can still walk," I say, before dragging them to their feet and giving them both a shove.

Pardoe again tries to take a swing at me.

For an instant, I feel like I'm back in the boxing gym. I duck the shot and pepper his body with a series of hard jabs before my nasty uppercut takes him off his feet again. That time, Pardoe stays down, muttering incoherently.

"Goodness gracious," says Phibe. "Where did you learn that?"

"In California," I say. "It's a bit rough out there."

Hany scowls at Chisholm, spitting toward him.

I lean threateningly at the soldier and blank out his memory of these people. "Get out of here and maybe I won't report you two for deserting."

He bows his head, collects Pardoe's semi-conscious hide, and helps the man walk off. Once they stumble out of sight into the trees, I spin back to Cumberland and dust myself off.

"All set."

"You are one interesting lady, Missus." Cumberland shakes his head.

I grin at him. "If you only knew."

Chapter Twelve

Two days of near constant walking later, the men shimmer and blur. Within seconds, the 'old white guy' illusions fade away, leaving them back to normal. Okay, wow. That was weird to watch. Then again, welcome to my life.

When all the shimmering and blurring is done, Catherine wraps her arms around Edwin, muttering how good it is to see him, as if he'd gone away for a while.

"We're not quite there yet," says Cumberland.

"Sorry," I say. Sadly, I know my unavoidable sleep habits have slowed them down or they might've made it to the safehouse before the magic wore off. Still, they have me. And that's better than nothing.

Fortunately, we only encounter a pair of farmers transporting a wagonload of produce, who both freak out at the sight of a pair of black men with rifles. It's a simple matter to send them on their way after making them forget seeing a small army of African people. And they're also kind enough to part with some vegetables, since none of the escapees have eaten anything in two days.

Late that afternoon, we wander down a long-ass dirt road with farm plots on both sides, approaching a rather large house out in the middle of a field. Miles of open fields and woodlands surround us on all sides; there's no one around to observe us approaching the house other than the occupants. Three young girls run around playing out front, the eldest not even twelve. She spots us coming and darts inside, calling for her papa. Though she doesn't sound alarmed at all, the people behind me become nervous.

As we approach the porch steps, a thirtyish man with auburn hair steps out in overalls and a white shirt. The tween girl, barefoot in a white dress, clings to his side, smiling.

The two smaller girls stare in awe at the rifles.

"Pardon the bother," says Cumberland. "We's wond'rin if y'all might spare two cups o' molasses."

The farmer tips his hat. "Come on around back."

We follow him along the length of the large house to the rear. There, he pulls open a cellar type door and ushers everyone inside. Once in the basement, he pushes a shelf to the side, grabs a coat hook on the wall, and swings open a hidden door to reveal a medium-sized room behind it with some cots and a simple table.

"Y'all can hide yourselves in here. We'll send word up to the next waystation to arrange passage." The farmer shakes hands with Cumberland, and surprisingly, makes no mention of the rifles.

One by one, the former slaves walk by, nodding their thanks my way.

"Burley Pinkham," says the man to me by way of greeting. "Since you don't need to stay out of sight, you're welcome to a room upstairs."

"Thank you kindly," I say, my Southern accent coming out unintentionally.

Burley chats with Cumberland, basically warning him that if outsiders come by, someone will tap on the floor as a warning for all to duck inside that hidden room and keep quiet. Since the property is isolated, there's no need for them to sit in there otherwise.

Soon, the escapees settle in for some much-needed rest, and I follow Burley back outside and around to the front of the house. He introduces me to his wife, Susanna, and their hired serving girl, a petite blonde named Lanie Oston. I learn that the Pinkhams have been assisting runaways headed north for some time now.

Later, once the food is ready, I help Lanie carry trays down to the former slaves. We talk on the way, and she tells me she used to live about a mile up the road, but became an orphan a year ago at fourteen. The Pinkhams half-adopted, half-hired her to work around the house. While she doesn't object to helping the slaves, she's terrified that doing so will get all of them killed.

The kids mob us when we enter the concealed room, jumping and reaching for the first real food they've probably ever smelled since arriving in the country. After getting everyone situated with their meals, Lanie and I head back upstairs to join the family and six workmen for supper. Their three daughters are remarkably quiet and well-mannered, but then again, I'm used to modern kids being annoyed with anything that pulls them away from their electronics. Anyway, the baked ham is quite good, even if my taste buds aren't terribly interested in real food, though I decline seconds since there's no point in wasting it.

When the meal's done, Burley and the workers head back outside to throw a few more hours' work on the farm. Susanna takes the girls off somewhere, and Lanie gets started gathering the dishes to wash. She looks utterly exhausted, so I get up and pat her on the shoulder.

"I can do this. You look like you're ready to collapse."

Lanie sighs and pulls a few stray strands of hair off her face. "It's no bother, ma'am. Gotta do my work."

It's so bizarre to see a girl Tammy's age behaving like an employee rather than a daughter, but I realize times are different and she actually isn't their child. Still, the mom part of me can't tolerate how exhausted she looks.

"I insist. You'll make yourself sick. Please rest and let me help a little. It's the least I can do for the hospitality."

Lanie sighs and looks at the floor. "All right, ma'am."

While I collect the dishes, she sets herself down in a chair adjacent to the door to the hallway and lets her head rest against the wall. The poor girl practically passes out as soon as her butt hits the cushion. Maybe ten minutes into washing dishes, a *crack* like someone hit the wall in front of me with a hammer accompanies a spray of splinters and a horrendous burning pain in my chest.

I peer down at a not-quite inch-wide hole in my chest at the base of my neck. My legs get weak, and for a second, my arms on the sink edge support more weight than my feet. The burning rod-like pain's a clear indicator that the bullet went clear through me. I'm pretty sure it didn't cut my spine since I can still feel my legs, even though they're not presently interested in supporting my weight. However, a couple of ribs have shattered, which hurts like hell.

All I can think about though is how Lanie is a bit shorter than me... if she'd been doing dishes, that bullet would've hit her right in the face. I shudder, more stunned at how close the girl came to death than being shot myself.

"Miss Moon!" gasps Lanie. She springs out of the chair and runs over to me, about to fly into a panic.

No one takes a hit like this and walks away alive... unless they're already dead. I swallow blood, unable to talk for a moment with a hole in my trachea. Fortunately, I don't need words for a mental command not to panic. Lanie stares at me with an expression I can only describe as constipated. Her desire to freak out crashes headfirst into my influence to stay calm. Neither of us says a word for a minute or so as the wound channel closes, leaving me bloodied but intact.

"Ouch," I mutter.

"Goodness," rasps Lanie, shaking. "You're shot."

A speck of metal on the dinner table catches my eye. The slug burrowed into the thick wood after coming out of my back.

"Miss Moon?" Lanie paws at my chest, gasping at the small hole in my dress. "H-how are you still standing?"

"I got lucky," I say, staring into her eyes. "The bullet came in the wall and missed me by inches."

Her eyes flutter. In flagrant disregard of the blood seeped into the fabric of my dress, she looks back and forth from the wall to the table. Then again, the fabric was already burgundy and already bloody as hell from my brief stint at nursing. "Lord have mercy! That almost hit you!"

There must be a battle going on quite a distance away since I can't hear the sounds of gunfire. Talk about a stray bullet from hell. I pluck the projectile out of the wood, surprised to see it's not a sphere but a round-nosed slug with a hollow end, somewhat deformed by passing through a wall and yours truly. The field doctors I 'worked' with grumbled about these. Minié balls or some such thing. They have a tendency to go clear through a body and smash bones, whereas the spherical musket balls often bounced off bone and wedged in muscle. Both surgeons hated the new ammunition since it caused more grievous wounds.

"Go collect the children. Bring them somewhere safe," I say.

Lanie nods and rushes off, shouting for the girls.

Again, I glance at my ruined dress. Hopefully, the lady of the house has something she can spare.

Chapter Thirteen

Susanna Pinkham "loans" me a simple sundress, likely something she'd wear only around the house and not out in polite company.

Okay, I swiped it. It was either that or explain the bullet hole. Of course, watching me essentially steal from the very people willing to risk their lives to help slaves amuses the hell out of Elizabeth. Though, technically I saved Lanie's life, albeit by total chance, so I don't feel too guilty about the dress. And she has quite a few similar garments; oh, and it's *much* less cumbersome.

Anyway, with Phibe and the rest of the people I'd been escorting now reasonably safe, I can return my attention to finding Delacroix and getting the hell out of the 1860s. Unfortunately, the Pinkhams put up a fuss when I try to thank them for their hospitality and head off in the middle of the night. Susanna is about to ask about the sundress, when I give her simple suggestion that she offered it to me. Sad thing is, I'm sure the woman would have let me have it if I'd asked. But I can't explain the hole.

So, I wind up sitting up all night in a room they insist I sleep in. Nothing makes time drag like wanting to be elsewhere in a hurry. Thoughts of Lanie almost eating a bullet mix with my home-sickness. Yeah, maybe a bit of crying happens. As much as Delacroix managed to convince me that my kids aren't experiencing time passing without me there, that doesn't mean *I* don't miss them. Time is still passing for me without them. Ugh. If this is a preview of what I'm going to be like when they're grown and moved out… I've been through some *wild* shit since becoming a vampire, but the hardest thing I'm ever going to face is having to let them be adults someday.

Eventually, the approaching sun knocks me out. To my perception, time jumps forward like six hours in an instant. After tidying the bed I slept in, I head downstairs to make pleasantries with the family. They're in a tizzy over the bullet that almost took Lanie's life, clearly far more worried about her than simple employers ought to be. Perhaps the employee part is a legal technicality so she can stay with them, but I suspect they really have more adopted her than anything. It's crazy to think that maybe all the work she does would be normal in this time period for a daughter that age. I can barely get Tammy to pick up her room.

I pop downstairs for a brief farewell with

Cumberland and the others. After wishing them safe travels north, I head out into another blistering late-August day. Soon after returning to the woods, I spot a giant buck, which I run down and feed from. One advantage to taking meals from large animals like cows and deer is, I don't have to worry about killing the poor things by drinking too much.

Since I could run all over the place hunting for Delacroix, and I know he's heading back to New York, the best plan I come up with over an hour of pacing around and grumbling to myself is to wait for dark and fly to New York. That will at least get me away from the Civil War. Of course, should something happen to Delacroix and he never makes it... well, I could spend years searching for him and not realize I'm wasting time.

Still, flying to New York is the best idea I've got. But I'm not about to take to the skies in broad daylight. Granted, there's no Internet here or legions of people with smartphones, so if anyone *did* see me, they'd probably be laughed off as drunks for telling anyone about a giant bat-dragon thing.

While debating whether or not I should wait for nightfall to take to the sky, George Clarke shimmers into being a few paces away, nearly invisible in the light of day.

Ugh. That poor boy.

He seems to pick up on my reaction and bows his head with a grateful expression. It must be lonely for him if he's thankful a total stranger feels horrible that he died. I can't think of anything to say, so we sit there in silence for a little while before he walks up to stand beside me.

"Miss Moon?" he asks. "I think you should follow me, quick-like."

I perk up. "What's wrong?"

"That man you're looking for." George points off to the side. "He's injured."

Damn. I stand. "What happened?"

George shrugs.

"How far?"

He scratches his head, glances off in the same direction, and shrugs again. "It's strange being a ghost, ma'am. Everything looks different. Can't rightly say how far, but I think you should be able to walk there."

"All right." No sense debating minutiae with a ghost, especially when my best chance for going home might be dying somewhere nearby.

George rushes off into the trees. In order to keep pace with him, I have to hike up this dress into a miniskirt. Not that anyone is likely to get a good view of my thighs with me running at a speed way faster than a human should be able to go, but I'm showing enough skin to cause a Southern Baptist to burst into flames. It's so damn nice to be free from that other outfit I'd been stuck in for days. Still, considering I got flung across time in my Talos form and landed in 1862 buck naked, I'll take a ridiculously overcomplicated dress over nothing. Though, it's been so damn hot lately, wearing nothing at all would probably still feel overdressed.

Honestly, I have no idea how people here tolerate this heat—especially without A/C.

Anyway, George blurs among the trees, his form having lost much of its humanlike shape. I fly as fast as I can make myself move on land, dodging around the forest, leaping creeks and streams. Almost an hour into the chase, I scare the absolute shit out of a pair of adolescent boys. Neither one of them react until I'm well into the trees on the other side, at which point they both scream at what had to be a blur of white fabric and dark hair.

I'm sure they're both running home to tell their mama about the 'ghost lady' or whatever they think blurred past them.

Okay, it's kinda mean of me to mentally laugh at that, but I've always had a thing for sneaking up and scaring people—especially my brothers. Dusk —yeah, his name is Dusk, and yeah, I had hippie parents—was always jumpy as a kid. I could get him to freak without even trying. Just walk up beside him and say 'hey,' and he'd practically jump out of his skin. Mary Lou, on the other hand, hardly ever batted an eyelash when I tried to get her. Once, I hid in her clothes hamper and shouted 'boo' when she lifted the lid. She threw her dress over my head and shut the lid on me. Killjoy. Got Dad once too, right when he started taking a hit off his bong. Scaring him made him inhale hard. Thought I damn near killed him the way he coughed and cursed.

Two hours into running, I start to wonder

exactly how distorted a perception of distance a ghost has. Right as I'm about to ask, George stops on a dime and I whoosh past him. It's not easy to go from a full-on vampiric sprint to a dead stop, so I slow down carefully. The last thing I need is to wipe out, shred this dress, and strand myself out in the sticks with nothing but cotton undergarments.

George waits for me by a large tree as I trot back to where he jammed to a halt. His expression is somber, but not so much that I jump to a worst-case assumption. Well, that, and there's no Delacroix ghost staring at me, which is damn good news.

A moan issues out from the underbrush.

I rush over, pulling vines and leaves aside.

Delacroix lays sprawled in a shallow gulley, roughed up and bleeding from several places. He looks like he got into a fistfight with five men.

"Jean," I say, pronouncing his name the French way, and kneel beside him.

He groans and shifts his gaze to me. A moment of panic comes and goes on his face, replaced with a resigned sense of 'screw it.'

"Miss Moon," he says. "Fancy meeting you here."

"What happened?" I check him over, but don't see any serious or obvious problems. No gunshots or stab wounds anyway.

"Couple of"—he coughs—"soldiers. Robbed me."

I hover over him, cradling his head in both

hands and stare into his eyes. When I spot Chisholm and Pardoe in his memory, the two idiots who attacked us a few days ago, I growl.

Delacroix shivers.

Oops. My growl's a bit low and, well, sounds more like a pissed-off lion than a woman.

"Calm down," I say. "I'm not angry with you. Those two jackasses who attacked you... I ran into them a while back." For once in my life, I almost regret *not* murdering people at random. Of course, how could I have known those two would come back to bite me in the ass.

"*Donc, voici comment ma vie se termine.*" He chuckles. "*Jamais je n'aurais imagine...*"

"Sorry. I have no idea what you said. I took Spanish in high school."

Delacroix shifts his head, staring up at me with a perplexed expression. "What is 'high school'? Is that something they have in California?"

"It's something they have in the future." I shake my head at him. "You shouldn't have run off. But I can't say I blame you. I'd probably run from a vampire, too."

"So, this is how it ends for me?" he wheezes.

"Not if I can help it." I scoop him up and stand, holding him. "You're still my ticket home. I was a little upset at you for that note, but I'll forgive you if you stay alive."

"Doing my best." He coughs again. "Those men were rather interested in my belongings."

Grumbling, I turn in place. Oh hell. As long as

I spent running, I've gotta be forty miles away from the Pinkhams' place; that is, if I can backtrack my way to it. And it's anyone's guess which way to Richmond. Grr.

I set Delacroix back on the ground. "Guess this is your lucky day."

He raises one finger. "I beg to differ."

When I begin to strip, both his eyebrows go up.

"Madame, certainly you're not…"

"I'm not. I just don't fancy destroying my only clothing. Do me a favor and pretend you're not seeing this, okay?"

"You are a sight no man could forget, *mademoiselle*."

I smirk while rolling my dress and undergarments together into a bundle around my boots and setting it on his chest.

"You might want to close your eyes then so you can savor the good memories. I'm about to get a little… less than beautiful." *No offense, Talos. I mean that in the sense of femininity.*

Eyes closed, I picture the flame in darkness and call out to my dragon friend across the worlds.

Delacroix emits a noise like a startled pigeon and promptly faints. That actually works.

I gather him as gently as possible in my talons and leap into the sky. There's no way I'm carrying him on foot over such a distance at a walking pace without hurting him more. He's in no shape to support himself, so this is our best chance.

Once I climb above the trees, I'm treated to a

beautiful panoramic view of Virginia. Richmond appears to be somewhere off to my right and a bit behind. From my vantage point, I can see skirmishes going on around the railroad junction, but I'm nowhere close enough to be at risk of catching a stray bullet or causing alcoholism in anyone who spots me.

Still, after spying the Pinkhams' farm, which is fairly simple due to the wide open fields around it, I dip back down close to the treetops to hide, and power forward. Delacroix comes to a few minutes later, takes note of his situation (flying in the talons of a half-dragon creature) and promptly faints again. Just as well. The poor man will likely be happier not having this memory.

Minutes later, I swoop in to a hover behind the barn, the leathery flapping of my wings spooking the horses inside. After setting Delacroix down as gingerly as I'm able, I pop back to my human self and drop into a crouch. While I'm trying to unfurl the bundle of dress, a small gasp comes from behind me.

The Pinkhams' youngest daughter, Violet, who's about five, stares at me from tall grass up to her shoulders. She evidently thinks a grown woman being outside with no clothes is hilarious as she lapses into giggles. I feel horrible for tinkering with the mind of a tiny child, but I don't need her saying awkward things later. Her giggling trails off into a mesmerized stare. Leaving her 'paused,' I hastily dress, then make sure she thinks she'd been laughing at seeing me trip and land on my butt.

Violet resumes giggling.

I pick Delacroix up and carry him around the barn, heading across the inner field to the main house. The other daughters are out front, Ginny, the nine-year-old, sitting on the stairs with a doll, and Esther, the eldest at eleven, on the porch swing, reading.

Susanna, their mother, sits nearby on a wicker chair. She hops up and rushes down the stairs. "Heavens to Betsy, what's happened?"

"This man is a friend of mine. He's been accosted by brigands."

She tilts her head at me.

Oops. Is 'brigands' appropriate for the 1860s, or did I just 'go medieval?'

"Men robbed him," I say hastily, "and gave him a beating."

"Bring him inside." Susanna leads the way, holding doors open as she goes.

Maybe she's looking at me weird since I'm carrying a grown man with ease. I ignore it and haul Delacroix inside, upstairs, and into a small guest bedroom where I ease him onto the bed and remove his boots and travel pack. Lanie arrives soon after with a bowl of water, and we spend a few minutes cleaning him up. At some point, Delacroix wakes with a gasp, staring at me as though I'm about to devour his heart.

His mind is already blocking out any memory of him witnessing Talos on its own, so I give it a little nudge in that direction.

"I'll bring some soup if that's all right," says Lanie as she stands.

Delacroix nods. "That would be lovely. Thank you."

I wait for her to leave the room, then sigh. "So that's what you're doing down here in Richmond… helping Cumberland and his family flee to the north."

"Yes." He coughs, winces, and clutches his side. Likely a broken rib. "The man's brother found me in New York, asked me to do what I could."

"They made it," I say. "I traveled with them to the safehouse." I'm not sure if Delacroix is supposed to know that we're technically *in* the same safehouse, so I don't mention it.

He blinks. "Surely, you jest. Even after the ensorcellment?"

"I had to do what I could." I chuckle. "Not all vampires are evil. I know why you think so, and the dark spirit inside me is probably as evil as they come… but I'm trying to contain her." I ramble for a bit about my struggles with Elizabeth, and mention again my alchemist friend, Max. "I think of it like fate chose me for the responsibility of containing her. I dunno. Maybe she won't bring about the end of the world, but I'm not ready to risk it."

Delacroix reaches over and takes my hand. For a moment, I think we're about to have a tender moment, but once again seems more interested in my 'eat food' ring. His gaze shifts to meet mine. "And I never would've imagined a crea—forgive me, a woman in your condition would be capable of anything but monstrosity."

"Thanks… I think. I couldn't just leave Cumberland and his family like that. It's not right how people are treated back here."

"Tell me it's changed in your time?" he asks in a weak rasp.

I fidget at my dress, picking lint and flicking it away. "I wish I could say it's perfect. It's not. There's still a lot of problems, but it's much better than it is here. The North wins the war and abolishes slavery, but prejudice is like a rich old mother in law… takes forever to die."

He starts to laugh but stops with a wince. "Ouch. It's good to know we prevail. How bad does it get?"

"The Civil War?"

"Yes."

"Pretty bad. I remember something about Sherman's march. They did a *lot* of damage to the South."

"An associate of mine—more charlatan than anything—is convinced Lincoln won't survive the war."

"He does die, yeah. Assassinated." I pick at my fingernails. "Sorry for not paying much attention in history class. I wanna say he was shot like a month or two before the Civil War officially ended, but I'm not a hundred percent sure of the date."

Delacroix chuckles. "Fancy that. All the spurious things my friend has tried to predict, and he winds up correct about something so major. I'm surprised you aren't tempted to stop it. The assassination, I mean."

"Well, for one thing, I'm from a world where it already happened. For another, there's a bit of 'not my problem' creeping in, and what if the timeline wants to preserve itself so Lincoln still dies from some other random thing."

He chuckles. "Perhaps anything you do here in the past will unwind when the spell is broken."

My heart ices over thinking of Lanie and her near-death experience at the kitchen sink. "Are you sure about that?"

"It's time travel. I'm sure of nothing. Though, I would wager that the more significant a disturbance, the greater the odds of things evening out."

"So, if I save the life of no one important in the grand scheme of world history, they'll stay alive, but if I kill Hitler, someone else will take that role."

"Who is Hitler?"

I shiver. "Someone who murdered millions."

He gawks. "How is that even possible, to kill on such a grand scale?"

"He rises to power in Germany and starts a war that involves most of the developed world. Uhh, France gets pretty chewed up, too. That's, of course, after the First World War."

"There are two such wars?"

"Yes."

Delacroix sighs.

"But we, I mean the good guys, win in the end… still, many, many innocent people die."

"It must be tempting for you to stay here in the past and change so much horror. Alas, I fear things will not quite work out as you hope in that regard."

"What about Lanie?" I ask in a whisper, lest someone in the house overhear, then explain the Minié ball that likely would've killed her.

"Unless she's going to do something significant, I doubt it." He coughs again, cringing in agony.

"You should rest."

Delacroix swats at my hand when I try to check on him. "Of course, I may well be completely off on a tangent. Perhaps you *can* alter the future."

"I'm really not that interested. Like it or hate it, the world I live in is the world I know. If I change too much, who knows what I'll go back to? The most important thing for me is getting home to my kids."

"There is a slight problem with that," he wheezes, then holds up his hand, revealing a band of pale skin on his finger. "Those ruffians took my ring."

"Your focus ring?"

"You remembered."

"Of course, I remembered. We need that ring."

"Yes," he said. "We do."

Chapter Fourteen

It's probably a good thing I don't have laser-beam eyes like Superman, or the Pinkhams wouldn't have a house anymore. It's also probably a good thing that those two Confederate deserters aren't anywhere near me right now or I'd do something rather unlike me.

"So… this ring is important?" I ask. "Nothing like it in New York?"

"Unless you don't mind a two-year wait while I attempt to craft another one."

"So, I need to find this ring."

"Very much so."

I sigh as Lanie walks in carrying a bowl of soup over to the bed. With great difficulty, Delacroix props himself up enough that she sets the tray across his lap. She sits on the edge of the bed, intent on feeding him.

"I can do that," I say. "I'm sure you've quite a

bit else to worry about."

"It's no bother, ma'am," says Lanie, looking at me like she'd get in trouble for not staying here.

I smile. "Well, I don't mean to chase you away. If you've nothing more pressing to attend to."

She exhales with relief. "Seeing after guests is my job, ma'am."

All three daughters hover at the door, curious about the guest. The sight of children simultaneously warms my heart and makes me homesick. They soon bore of watching Lanie feed Delacroix, who appears to enjoy not having to move much more than his jaw.

Once the soup is gone, Lanie stands with the tray and peers at me. "Anything else I can help with?"

"It might be wise to send for a doctor if there's any to be found given the war," I say.

Lanie gives me the same 'yeah, right' look Tammy often does, though she'd be perplexed by that phrase. I guess some things remain true for teens regardless of era. "I will tell Mr. Pinkham about his condition, ma'am."

"Thank you."

After she breezes out of the room, I glance again at Delacroix's hand. "So, that ring is critical?"

"In and of itself, it can be used to dispel minor magical effects. Especially charms."

I squint at him, playfully annoyed. "So you…"

"Broke free from your compulsion within minutes, but pretended to be under your influence until a suitable distraction presented itself." He smiles. "I would chuckle, but I fear the pain would be too great. Forgive my deception."

"Right. So the ring removes magic."

"Minor magic."

"But it's not powerful enough for what sent me back here."

"Precisely." He shifts his eyes toward me. "I sense you are about to ask if I can elsewise render the magic upon you ineffective without the ring. It is possible, though I suspect it would be far easier for you to locate an already existing mechanism—the ring, I mean—by which I can guarantee success than for me to spend the next several years fiddling about with experiments attempting to recreate it."

"Fair enough. And you're sure that it will work to simply remove the magic?"

"Quite." He raises a hand to his face, muffling a cough. "The magic affecting you... think of it like wrapping a rock in a sheet of silk, and pushing it through a hole in a fence. The fence represents your time. The space behind the fence represents the past. The rock, of course, is you. Even though the rock would be in the space behind the fence, it remains wrapped in the silk."

"And the silk is the magic in this analogy."

"Indeed." He next makes a drawing-apart gesture with both hands. "Now, pull the silk back through the hole, the rock returns to your present. That ring, along with a sufficiently powerful source of magic focused through it, will snap your silk back through the hole and catapult you to approximately the instant you left."

I raise both eyebrows. "Approximately?"

He shrugs, cringing from pain. "This is all out of my field of expertise. Had I not met you, I scarcely would have believed traversing time even possible."

"What if the ring just cuts a hole in the silk and the rock drops out?"

He shakes his head. "No, that would be opening the threads of the enchantment. Completely different than canceling it entirely. And we will need more than the ring. The problem is, my power source is back in New York. And even that may not be strong enough to break this enchantment."

"I won't pretend I understand that... but I'll trust you."

"Trust is tricky, Sam. Were I not unable to move, I still might be tempted to flee from your presence. However, I suppose after what you've done for Cumberland and the others, I should at least render the benefit of doubt. You have had ample time to do unseemly things to me, and haven't."

"Thanks." I glance over at him. "Do you know anything about glowing paths?" I explain about Chloe and what she said about five paths meeting and the image in her head of me walking on a dirt road made of glowing blue energy.

His expression is probably the same one that had been my face while staring at that woman. The look he gives me fits my father's voice asking, "What drugs are you on and can I have some?"

"Guess not." I sigh. "All right. I'll find that ring."

He nods.

"Need anything before I go?"

"Just rest."

"All right. I'll get started."

He closes his eyes and lets out a belabored groan as I make my way out of the room and go downstairs. Lanie runs over to me in the hall, tears streaming from her eyes, and grabs me like I'm her long-lost mother returning from a ten-year absence.

"Umm…"

She sobs on my shoulder for a little while before collecting herself. "Forgive me, ma'am. I was in the kitchen cleaning up, and I saw the hole in the wall. Right as high as my head. If you hadn't insisted on helping me last night, I would… I would…" She shivers.

Mom time. I pat her back and mutter the same sort of reassurances I used to use when Tammy had nightmares. "It's better not to think about what might've been."

My brain randomly leaps to my conversation with Delacroix and bounces from there back to history class. Something about a young woman being killed in her home by a stray bullet during the Civil War. I start to worry that I'm responsible for a major alteration of history, but then it hits me that the woman I'm thinking of had been in Gettysburg... and probably hasn't died yet since it's too early on in the war.

What are you waiting for then, Sssamantha? asks the slithery voice in my head. *Bessst hurry on to Gettysburg and sssave another hapless innocent.*

I smirk. Okay, so I *do* feel a little guilty about not being interested in doing that, but I need to go home. I'd rather not wait the few years until then. Plus, how would I, other than by sheer random chance, stop *another* person from being caught by a stray bullet? Critical information like the exact date and time is not in my head. I couldn't really save her if I wanted to.

"I can't believe how close I almost came to dying," mutters Lanie, still sniffling. "I'm sure my ma and pa sent you here to protect me."

Somehow, I doubt her ma is a voodoo priestess in my time. Still, if it comforts her, let her think that. "I bet they're watching over you."

She gives me a teary smile. "Are you leaving already again?"

"I must. I've some important business to attend." I squeeze her hand. "But I'll return soon. Please pass along my thanks to the Pinkhams for their hospitality and for helping my friend, Mr. Delacroix."

"Please be careful. It's ungodly out there, ma'am. Oh, what's the nation coming to when a girl can't even clean dishes without worrying for her life?"

"Sounds like South Central," I mutter.

"Pardon?" asks Lanie.

"Nothing." I wince. "You're right. The country has lost its sanity for sure."

She hugs me again. "I'll go let Mr. Pinkham know to fetch a doctor if he can."

"Thank you."

Lanie hurries off into the house. I head out the front door and sigh at the setting sun.

No big deal. I just have to search all of Virginia for a pair of Confederate deserters. And that's if they haven't already pawned the ring.

I sigh again.

Chapter Fifteen

Once again, I find myself flying.

At least at the moment, the cover of darkness helps. I'm not entirely sure what I'd expected to find by zigzagging back and forth in midair, yet here I am doing it. A few lone campfires draw my curiosity, though none of them turn out to be the dynamic duo. They didn't take Delacroix's traveling bag, which, come to think of it, did kinda feel empty. I'm sure they had little interest in common clothing, even the fancy stuff. Their loss. Who knows what else might've been in there. Either way, that ring would sell for a decent amount all by itself.

I've seen enough Westerns to get the feeling these two are probably either on their way to Mexico to avoid being executed for deserting or heading to the nearest brothel. Perhaps both. Then again, this isn't exactly the modern era. How likely are they to be identified as deserters? If pressed, they could fall into another company with false names or lie and say they got separated from their unit. No guarantee they'd be fearing the consequences of fleeing. Which makes it even more likely they'd stop somewhere to, um, *exploit* their sudden reversal of fortune.

A few hours into my search, a grouping of fires close together in the distance gives away the location of a military encampment. At this point in the war, any military camp in Virginia is going to be Confederate. While I highly doubt the two men I'm looking for are there, it's worth checking anyway on the off chance they changed their minds or repatriated when cornered. If they haven't, perhaps I can find someone who knows them. They might even be heading home in hopes their families will hide them.

Anyway, I land a safe distance from the camp, which from the air looks reasonably large, a couple thousand men at least. Once I'm shapeshifted back to normal and dressed, I sneak through the woods until I happen upon a perimeter sentry. For a moment, I consider mesmerizing him and stealing his uniform to walk around, but for one thing, he stinks, and for another, I'm not a mortal anymore. Disguises are for chumps. Or lesser beings. And, I also doubt anyone here would buy a woman in a soldier's uniform.

He scrambles to get his rifle up in time to point at me as I step out in front of him, but I zip into his face much faster than he can react, one hand over his mouth.

"Shh," I say. "I'm just a li'l bitty woman all alone in the woods. Nothing to be afraid of."

The man relaxes.

I remove my hand from his mouth. "I'm trying to find a couple of soldiers. Do you know Alton Chisholm or Fred Pardoe?"

His thoughts are genuinely blank as he shakes his head.

"Drat." I leave him staring into space, after wiping the memory of his having seen me.

The sentry doesn't twitch for a good three minutes. By the time he resumes his perimeter walk, I'm near the outer array of tents. Between my heightened senses of hearing and smell, it's not terribly difficult to know when people are coming and going. For now, I duck out of sight between the white canvas walls.

All around me, men laugh, snore, belch, and gossip. Several talk about how General Lee is feeling his oats after routing General Pope at Bull Run while protecting Manassas Junction, and they're floating rumors that Lee's contemplating a northward push. The Confederates are riled up with excitement at the idea of not only protecting the South, but *invading* the North. Thankfully, at least there's a few dissenters who grumble about the whole war being pointless or tragic... but the 'Sovereign South' crowd is way louder.

For the better part of an hour, I creep around

out of sight. It really illustrates how "normal" vampires have such an easy time ambushing people for feeding. I mean, I get that these guys aren't really trained soldiers like I'm used to thinking of trained soldiers, but it's sinfully easy to avoid detection. And sure, I have gone through Quantico and I've got superhuman senses and reflexes, but *still*. It feels like I'm tiptoeing around a camp full of visually impaired people. Most of them are sitting around fires, staring into the flames, which destroys their night vision. The ones who aren't mesmerized by burning wood are either sleeping or walking perimeter guard. Unfortunately, none of them— either subconsciously or consciously—know either man I'm looking for.

I approach a few lone sentries or soldiers on their way to/from the latrine pit. And no, it doesn't smell much better at night. Rotting urine still stinks to high heaven. Yes, I just said high heaven. I swear, if I make it home, I'm going to spend six hours in a bubble bath. And that's *still* not going to make me feel clean.

I head along a row of tents near the eastern edge of the camp, peering inside the quiet ones on the off chance one of the deserters is there, but I'm not that lucky. The ninth tent I check, I wind up nose-to-pistol with a fortyish man in his undershirt and shorts. He's as stunned to see a woman as I am to see a potbellied guy in the closest thing 1862 has to a tank top and tightie-whities. If not for a ball-and-cap revolver in my face, I might've laughed at such a rounded torso with stick legs.

He's also got one of those super-bushy mustaches that wraps around his cheeks and connects to the hair by his ears.

"Hello," I whisper. "Sorry to bother you. You can put the gun down now."

The man lowers his arm, the confusion in his expression deepening. He can't quite understand why he's listening to me.

"Thank you. Do you know a pair of soldiers named Alton Chisolm or Fred Pardoe?"

I nearly yelp in delight when his thoughts jump straight to the two "layabouts" as he thinks of them.

"Yeah. Ain't with this unit, but I know 'em. Boys came from farms down by Suffolk. Be a dang miracle if they're not dead yet. Neither one what could figure out the proper end of a gun ta point at the Yanks." He proceeds to grumble about the recruitment standards of the Confederate Army, or lack thereof. In his opinion, the only bar one had to pass to be enlisted was having two arms, two legs, two eyes, and two testicles—brain optional. "Them boys figure they join up and get all kinds o' women. Neither one o' them much cottoned on ta what it really meant bein' a soldier."

"Right." I nod. "I got that feeling. So, you haven't seen them?"

"Why, one of 'em the daddy?"

I roll my eyes. "Please. I have standards. No, they did, however, steal something of mine."

"What in tarnation is a lady doin' out here

lookin' for thieves—not that I put it past them lot—
but another thing, what's a lady doin' runnin'
around out here at night? How'd you get in the
camp past the sentries?"

"There's sentries?" I ask, feigning innocence.

His face turns red. "Blast it all. If Hanrahan's
fallen asleep again, so help me!"

"Calm down."

My command settles him in an instant. The
sergeant stares at me with almost the exact same
expression Anthony used to have as a baby while
watching me prepare his bottle. After reading his
mind to get a sense of where Suffolk is, I dive a
little deeper and make sure he thinks he only
dreamed seeing me, since, after all, a lady wouldn't
possibly be roaming around at night or have made it
past their excellent sentries.

"Go back to sleep," I whisper and duck out of
the tent.

I resist the urge to grumble at the whole
'helpless little lady' thing until I'm far enough away
into the woods that no one will hear me.
Considering this guy thinks of the two men I need
to find as lazy good-for-nothings, it's a fair bet they
simply got tired of the army being more than they
bargained for. Maybe they even went home. If
they're really as dumb as that sergeant thinks, they
probably did just that.

May as well head to Suffolk.

Chapter Sixteen

With the knowledge I skimmed from the sergeant, I get my bearings and head off into the forest.

For once, my being forced to stay awake when the sun's down is a benefit. Technically, I don't get tired. Whether I sit on my ass all night long or sprint doesn't make a difference. I think that's one of the parts of being a vampire that took the most getting used to. Especially after all the physicality my former job with HUD required. Well, more the training to get the job. The *actual* job tended to involve powerlifting staplers more than anything else. I'm so used to being winded after running that now as a vampire when I'm not, my brain plays tricks on me sometimes and tricks me into thinking I'm out of breath.

Weird, I know. Welcome to my world.

That said, oncoming sunrises create a sensation

similar to exhaustion. But again, it doesn't matter how much or little I did in the hours leading up to that—I get the same sense of tiredness and agitation. So there's no point in me trying to save energy. Of course, other than Suffolk, I don't have a specific destination in mind, so there's also no need to sprint. I move through the woods at a brisk jog while keeping my senses as open as possible. Not that I expect either of those two men to be anywhere within spitting distance of a Confederate Army encampment, but if I've learned anything in my adult life, it's never to underestimate the power of stupid.

People do some *dumb* things sometimes.

Like fill out forms for HUD assistance and use two different names on the *same* set of documents. It's a pretty good indicator that someone's using a fake identity when they keep forgetting their supposed name.

Anyway…

A good while after leaving the army camp behind, George Clarke—or rather, his ghost—steps out of the trees and walks by my side. It's almost not horribly depressing to see him. Almost. At least I don't break out into tears when he offers a feeble smile of greeting.

"Still here in your past?" asks George.

"There have been… complications."

"Complications?"

"Two of them." I grumble to myself for a few seconds, then sigh. "The men who attacked Delacroix, that man you helped me find, robbed him." I explain the ring and how important it is to my going home. "I hate to say it, but maybe I should've roughed them up a bit more when they menaced Hany and those people. Letting them live is probably only going to guarantee they hurt some other innocent person."

George stares at me with hazel eyes far too innocent to belong to a ghost. "It's not in you to kill if you can help it, ma'am. But, I fear they're not long for this world."

"What? They're dying?" I slow to a walk and stare at him.

"Them two men should'a been dead when they attacked those slaves. If you'da not been here, they would'a been traveling without an escort. Phibe dun took a fatal shot tryin' ta protect the younger one, an' the men would'a beat the two deserters plum dead. You bein' there kept three souls outta death's claws, but they's all fated to die."

"I don't believe in fate." I gaze off into the forest, my vampiric eyes peeling away the shadows.

George shrugs. "S'pose that's your thinkin'. But feels like there's somethin' outta balance 'round you."

I chuckle. "That's putting it mildly."

"Forgive me, ma'am. My head's all still a bit addled from being dead and all."

"Yeah. Takes a while to get used to, or so I'm told." I also suspected I was only speaking to an aspect of George Clarke, a sort of split energy. His real self—his actual soul—was long gone.

He cocks his head at me in confusion for a few seconds before understanding spreads over his features. "About them two deserters, bein' a ghost an' all, feels like they missin' from here. An' somethin' ain't rightly likin' it."

"George…I can't randomly murder them because 'it's supposed to happen.'"

"You ain't from this place. Best not be changin' too much."

I watch my boots eat up the terrain for a silent few minutes, debating with myself if I have it in me to "set the universe right" if that means killing two men, unsavory as they may be. I'd most certainly not be able to kill Lanie, and not even those two idiots. About the only way I could ever see myself coming unglued enough to commit actual murder would be exacting revenge on someone who even threatened Tammy or Anthony, let alone something worse. Of course, I made short work of an asshole named Ira Levine, who threatened my kids a few years back. Not even prison could keep him safe from me.

I stop walking and close my eyes. *And so help me, if I even think you ever had anything to do with hurting them, I'm going to fling myself into the sun without this ring on.*

I amend that and think: *After I tear to pieces whoever harmed them, of course.*

Elizabeth writhes in the back of my mind. She doesn't speak, but I get the feeling she's trying to remind me of the truce she accepted soon after I woke as a vampire. My kids are off-limits. I'll never forget how horrified I was that day when four-year-old Tammy smelled so appetizing. She crept into the bathroom after the first of many meltdowns I'd have over my death and hugged me, trying to make me feel better. Her neck—so close to my face—set off an explosion of hunger and horror.

"What will happen if I don't kill them?" I ask.

George, hands in his trouser pockets, shrugs. "I don' reckon entirely, but I figure they both marked as havin' cheated death. Bad fortune might could find them n'matter what you do. Likely soon."

"Does their not being dead harm you in any way?" I ask.

"No." George smiles. "I'm still hangin' 'round ta help you, ma'am. Seein' as how ya took so kindly ta tryin' ta tend ta me. Reckon I'll be here 'til yer affairs are settled."

I chuckle. "You're going to be waiting a while. I'm not planning on dying any time soon… again."

"Oh…" He tilts his head at me. "Not meanin' yer goin' ta the next world. Meant getting' back ta yer time. I know what y'are, ma'am. Kin see it clear as you kin see me. My pa used ta talk 'bout things like that, but none of us ever believed him. Kinda surprised you ain't wanna kill them two, truth be told."

"Yeah, well… I'm full of surprises."

George laughs. "Aye, ma'am. I do rightly appreciate what you did for me. Them two men yer lookin' after is holed up in the town o' Chesterfield, enjoyin' their loot."

"Wow. I guess they're dumb *and* predictable. Brothel?"

You know what's weird? Watching a ghost blush.

"Aye, ma'am."

"All right. Which way to Chesterfield?"

George points. "That way, ma'am. Reckon I could show ya if ya like."

"That would be mighty kind of you." I try to pat him on the back, but my hand passes through him.

He ignores the attempt, nods, and marches off toward Chesterfield.

I know my being here didn't cause his death, but I still feel guilty. Maybe the problem with our country is how many of us sleep through history class. This kid's not even seventeen yet and he died for what he believes in (even if those beliefs happen to be backward). Tammy thinks the worst thing in the world is if one of the bands she likes is late in releasing their new album.

How times have changed.

At least Anthony's not a drama king.

Though he's been awful quiet lately. Ugh. I need to get home. Stat.

Chapter Seventeen

Dawn approaches right as I reach Chesterfield.

Great timing. I drag myself over to the nearest house and break into their cellar. Once inside, I take refuge on the bottom shelf below a stockpile of canned fruit that could keep the Confederate Army going for a month. An empty burlap sack makes for a decent bit of concealment. With any luck, no one will notice me in the few hours it takes my forced sleepiness to come and go. Not like I breathe, make any noise, or move at all.

Just a corpse to the rest of the world, I think sleepily. *Albeit, a cute and spunky one.*

It seems as though my eyes close and open in seconds. The only clue that time passed is the former silence is now full of cats yowling and an older woman's voice trying to calm them down. Great, the first house I pick and it's the Crazy Cat Lady of 1862. And her furry companions smell something dead in the basement. Not that I stink. Well… I do… but that's from not having a damn bath in weeks. Being undead, my body doesn't produce the same sorts of things-that-can-smell like it used to, but there's still some degree of it. Sweltering heat and wearing the same clothing for days in a row doesn't help.

But no, the cats aren't picking up my physical stink. They're sensing Elizabeth—or at least my undeadness.

Right. Time to get out of here before the old lady comes downstairs.

I kick out of the burlap, lofting a huge cloud of dust into the air, and stand. No sense raising a panic, so I wad up the fabric and toss it out of sight in the corner, then make my way up the cellar stairs outside. And ugh. It's not even noon yet and it's already as muggy as my bathroom after a long hot shower. I spend a moment swatting dust from my dress, grateful for the simpler garment. Today is going to be hotter than hell.

Chesterfield isn't a big town. It only takes me about ten minutes to locate the brothel, which is pretending to be a respectable boarding house. The three-story white building looks like a massive private home or a small hotel. It's also a touch on the creepy side, like the sort of place they'd use to film a ghost movie. A huge front porch with dark hardwood boards has several rocking chairs and small tables, none of which hold anything but air at the moment. A pair of double doors with plenty of window does make it look more like a business than a residence.

Signage on the front announces rooms for rent, by the night, week, or month. Yeah, right. I doubt many people use this place for long-term lodgings. That's likely only there to appease the town council or whoever else might take issue with having an establishment like this within walking distance of the town square.

I get a few disapproving looks from nearby pedestrians as I walk up onto the porch. Obviously, there's only one reason a young woman (or at least someone who appears to be an attractive-enough young woman) would go into this place. Oh, I couldn't possibly be hunting for a runaway husband, or here to drag my brother home—no, everyone assumes I'm looking for work. Whatever. Not like I'll have to ever see any of those judgmental pricks again. And I doubt any one of them would believe I'm a thirty-one-year-old mother of two. Okay, not everything about vamp- irism sucks.

Just the feeding.

Hah.

Anyway... I stroll into a parlor full of wingback chairs and divans that all appear fancy and about thirty years old. Great, this is like the secondhand store of booty. There's only one other person in the room, a late-thirties woman with black hair sitting behind an attempt at a hotel reception desk. She's more or less asleep, but stirs a little at the sound of my boot heels on the floorboards.

"I'm looking for two men," I say to the bleary-eyed woman, and peek into her head. "A pair of soldiers."

She remembers them with little opinion attached, though thinks of Pardoe as humorously charming. "Umm. Forgive me, Miss…?"

"Passing through." I smile and give her a prompt. "Which room or rooms are they staying in?"

"They booked room twelve for the night."

"Thank you kindly, Miss." I nudge her back asleep and remove myself from her memory.

My stomach rumbles. Damn. It's been a while since I've fed. That can wait the few minutes or so it will take me to finish up in here. I'm sure there's a cow or horse somewhere in Chesterfield willing to help me out, even if it doesn't want to.

After helping myself to the bundle of keys on the desk in front of her, I swoop around a pair of cream-colored divans and head up an ornate staircase to the second floor. One thing about the past—the buildings are beautiful. None of those cheap corner-cutting monopoly houses that developers put up by the dozens.

And yeah, this is *definitely* the kind of place that should be harboring more than a few ghosts. Though, considering I'm currently in 1862, perhaps those ghosts haven't been killed yet. Creepy old houses don't come with hauntings from the moment they're built. The corridor is remarkably clean, with ornate wallpaper and white-painted doors. Small, black hand-painted numbers identify the rooms.

Room twelve is at the far end of the hall, the door facing me instead of on either side. Once there, I start working my way through the keyring until I find the one that opens the lock. It's a large room with two beds and a tiny fireplace. A collapsible privacy barricade leans against the wall on the left by a small wardrobe cabinet. Pardoe and Chisholm are both sound asleep and mercifully covered up by their bedclothes. Though, Pardoe looks like he's come down with a bit of nasty fever. Fate seriously doesn't mess around.

While I don't need to worry about such things, I still give him a wide berth and proceed to rummage the room. Other than a stack of Confederate paper money, which even now is of dubious worth, they don't have anything that appears to belong to Delacroix. My expectation that they likely sold the ring and went straight to the nearest pub or brothel appears to have been proven true. Damn.

I grab Chisholm by a fistful of chest hair and shake him until he comes around. He stares foggily up at me for a few seconds before a dumb grin spreads over his lips. Oh, he thinks I'm here to entertain him. The anger radiating from my eyes chases his smile away in seconds.

"Who the hell are you?" he asks.

"You don't remember me?" I tsk at him. "I'm hurt."

He squints. Somewhere, deep in his brain, a thought-mouse scurries around a giant empty chamber hunting for a crumb, but doesn't find anything. Undoubtedly, they'd been a little drunk when they attacked the escaped slaves. Chisholm doesn't even remember the ass-kicking I delivered to his associate.

"No, but you's a mighty fine piece."

I wish I still had my Glock. I'd show him what a piece *really* is. "You attacked a man and stole several things from him. Where is his ring?"

The name Abner Wilkins flashes across his mind.

He squints at me, yawns, then mutters, "What ring?"

"Who is Abner Wilkins?" I ask.

Chisholm blinks. Some of the hangover-red fades from his cheeks. He's afraid to say anything right away, but his thoughts give away the general store in town. "I... umm... sold it. Thing paid for the best night of mah life."

I look around at the disheveled room, uniforms and underthings littered around, empty bottles on the nightstand, and the stink of sweat in the air. "You've had a sad life if this is the peak."

He stares at me, blank-faced.

Pardoe gurgles in his sleep, launching into a series of phlegmatic coughs. The wad of mucous doing backflips in his throat brings my mind around to what George Clarke said about these two having one foot in the grave already. While the ghost didn't

166

explicitly say he thought I *should* kill them, the implication hung there anyway.

I frown at Chisholm. They may be unsavory, and perhaps the world wouldn't miss them, but I'm not Fate's assassin. Shaking my head, I leave the men to their beds and head downstairs. The woman at the front desk doesn't notice me return the keys, nor does she stir as my boots *thunk* across the floor to the exit.

Oppressive heat slaps me in the face when I reach the street. I squint at the near-cloudless sky and the fuming ball of pain and suffering hanging in the air. Or, as some call it, the sun. Who's to say that any of what happens is preordained? I reckon if Fate existed, those two clowns would already be goners.

A sigh leaks out my nose. I seriously just used 'reckon' and not on purpose.

Yeah. I really need to get my ass home.

And not just my ass. All of me.

Chapter Eighteen

Once I'm out of the vicinity of the brothel, passing townsfolk's dark looks and head-shaking gives way to smiles and polite nods.

I do, however, get a few lingering stares. While I'm not entirely sure about the social mores of 1862 and what wearing a plain sundress out and about town could potentially imply about me, I like to think that the other women bustling about in their layers and layers are simply jealous. They don't have to know that the reason I'm not dripping with sweat is I have no body temperature.

I mean, my body *can* sweat, but it usually doesn't unless I overexert myself like at the gym. And, as best I can figure out, that only happens because I subconsciously think it ought to. One of those "trying to appear normal and blend in" things.

Oh, and contrary to what you might hear in certain parts of Southern California, clamping one's lips around a cow's neck is *not* "trying to appear normal and blending in." That's not going to happen in plain sight. It's a lot easier to lure a person into a secluded spot for feeding than it is to sweet-talk a cow into a hotel room—so I need to find a source of food that's already in an out-of-the-way place.

Though, honestly, drinking blood right from a live cow or horse is significantly tastier than the stuff I get in modern times that's been drained from an already-dead animal. Of course, I can't argue the convenience of feeding in the privacy of my annoyingly detached garage. My best chance to find an inconspicuous meal is not happening inside town. I'll deal with Abner Wilkins first and grab a bite at one of the outlying farms.

The Chesterfield General Store is like something out of a low-budget Western movie. In a hundred years, this store would undoubtedly be filled with Twinkies and Slurpee machines. For now, I head past shelves of various items, mostly in tins or jars, and approach the counter along the left side of the room. The man behind it is somewhere between over-the-hill cowboy and retired Confederate Army soldier. Pale blue shirt, gray trousers, long brown hair, fluffy mustache tinged with silver, and a black ten-gallon hat.

Oy. I gotta remember this is normal here. Back home, I'd be snickering under my breath at this getup.

"Can I help ya, missus?" asks the man.

"You Abner Wilkins?"

His eyes narrow. "Who's asking?"

"Just little ol' me," I say, trying to convey friendliness. "Some rather unscrupulous individuals stole something of mine and have confessed to selling it to you. I'm looking for a thick-banded gold ring with an interesting pattern… oh, and a red opal."

Abner's mustache twitches side to side. I half expect him to start singing *Froggy Went A-Courtin'*, but he only sighs. "Sorry, missus. Ya missed it by a couple hours. Thing caught the eye of a young corporal, bought it right up earlier this mornin'."

Eyes closed, I lean my head back and seethe in silence. This poor guy doesn't deserve my wrath.

"You all right, missus? Bit of heat out there today."

I stare at him. "It's important that I find this ring. What can you tell me about the man who purchased it? Where is he going?"

"Hmm." Wilkins rubs his chin. "Think the man's name was Cokely. Godfrey Cokely or somethin' of that nature. That ring of yours caught his eye right quick like, an' he figured it a good-luck charm. Light-haired man, 'bout your age. P'raps even as old as twenty-five."

"Oh, pshaw," I say, feigning a blush. "You're too kind. Do you reckon where he went?"

Abner raises an eyebrow. Wow, he really thinks I'm like twenty or so. Must be his age showing. I know the feeling. The older I get, the more adults younger than me look like kids. "Uhh, the boys took off outta here like a bat outta hell. Headin' northward. They's gonna give them Yanks the what for."

Dammit! I'm going to be chasing this stupid ring around so long I might as well just head out to California and bide my time until the calendar catches up. Blinding frustration triggers a rush of bad thoughts, everything from kicking over these shelves to tearing out Abner's throat.

Whoa.

Slow down there, Sam. That's Elizabeth talking.

"Heh," says Abner, reacting to the visible anger on my face. "I get riled up jes' hearin' the word 'Yanks,' too."

I give him the side-eye. "Yeah... So this Cokely left town with a lot of men?"

"Yes'm. The whole lot of 'em came up from Carolina what I hear."

"And they left town this morning?" I ask.

He nods. "Yes'm."

Well, a large number of soldiers can't be *that* difficult to find.

"Thank you kindly."

I scan his thoughts thoroughly, in particular, the youngish, handsome face that keeps popping up in Abner's forethoughts with every mention of Cokely's name. Once I've committed the face to memory, I offer a slight nod and hurry out.

Roughly ten minutes outside of Chesterfield

proper, I stray onto a small farm where some cows graze a good distance away from any buildings… or a chance of detection. Careful to watch my step for dung (which is easier to find if I listen for flies) I make my way across the meadow to the edge of a small wood line where the animals congregate in the shade. A bee goes by that looks big enough to carry mail.

I shudder. Wow. All the bizarre things I've tangled with since becoming a vampire and a giant bee *still* unnerves me.

An exceptionally loud *wswswsws* noise from some other insect deeper in the woods fills the air. Cows flick their tails at flies, a few of which come over to check me out but don't stay long. There in the bug-infested shade of a sunbaked field, I mind-whammy a cow so it stands there and lets me drink a pint or two. Though the blood is more fulfilling when fresh, I still get the sense that Elizabeth squirms at the thought of feeding from an animal. Drinking from bottles or cups is more "refined," or at least it allows a degree of separation from the reality of where the blood came from. To her, what I'm doing now is like a human eating cat food from a plastic dish on the floor.

With my lips pressed to a furry cow-neck, there's no denying what I'm eating. Of course, she thinks this is beneath her. Well, you should've picked a girl with a flimsier mind, one she could have long-since controlled. I wonder if she really expected someone like me, once part of a hereditary line of alchemists and consistently reborn as a witch, would be weak-willed? Then again, that's exactly why she picked me.

And we have all the time in the world, Sssamantha.

And there's the creepy bitch we all know and love, I think, and shove her deeper into my mind. This time I imagine a vast, bottomless pit.

Yes, Elizabeth probably expected I would have been a tough nut to crack. No doubt she believes she will break me eventually.

We'll see, I think... and cover the pit opening with a massive, mental vault.

For now, I pat the cow on the flank to calm it. Maybe I *am* demeaning myself by drinking cow blood, but hey...

Beef.

It's what's for dinner.

Chapter Nineteen

So, yeah. The cows and I have some quality time together.

I'm starting to respect them a lot more than I used to. Bees, not so much. Oh, they leave me alone all right, but it still makes my skin crawl when a weaponized insect big enough to have landing lights cruises by. The cows have also inspired me to de-stress as much as I can, which involves a combination of working smarter not harder, trying (futilely) to avoid worrying myself to death, and sitting on my ass until the sun goes down.

I can walk for hours and get hot, sweaty, and miserable—or I can fly after dark. Granted, I *could* fly right now if I wanted to. Talos can come out to play whenever I ask him to. But I'm also allergic to Minié balls. Not that I'm worried on an individual level about a bullet or two, but if I swoop in over a battle in progress, something tells me that *both* sides would suddenly forget their differences long enough to light me up. Getting shot once or twice is annoying but I'll deal. A few *thousand* hitting me at once? That might actually sting. And I'm pretty sure Talos isn't undead. That might actually kill him. And that's not something I'm prepared to risk. Not when all it costs me is a little waiting.

Considering I'm going to need to get undressed anyway, I peel off my boots and socks to enjoy a lazy afternoon-into-evening talking to the cows while wandering barefoot around the grass. This, of course, necessitates extra vigilance insofar as animal crap goes. It's almost impossible to actually *enjoy* the scenery as I leap from worrying about my kids to worrying about Delacroix to worrying about what if I never find this damn ring. The longer it takes me to track it down, the more I think Delacroix's going to get over his bruises and take off. I can't help but expect I'm going to get back to the Pinkhams' house and experience another crushing disappointment.

That man is morbidly afraid of vampires. And, well, if he *is* an agent of the light, that makes sense. Apparently, I'm not typical of my kind. I suppose it really boils down to if his desire to have this ring back outweighs his fear of what he thinks I could potentially do to him. And despite his reassurances that time isn't passing in the future, I can't go five minutes without thinking of Tammy and Anthony. I mean sure, they're not small children anymore and if something horrible happened to me, it's not as if they'd be helpless. Mary Lou will look after them, but she's not equipped to handle the sort of next-level bullshit that life's been throwing our way these days.

I can just picture the look on her husband's face if, say, a werewolf howled outside their front door. That might even get him to peel his eyes away from football. Not that Rick's *that* kind of man. He's a great husband and father, but he likes his football. Of course, one of those howling horrors walks into their house, I can just see him saying, "Nah, screw that," getting in the car, and driving until the tank runs out of gas.

Great husband and father…yeah, I once believed I'd found one of those, too. I thought Danny loved me. And maybe that was the real problem all along. He loved me *too* much to handle what happened. The man never could get over that whole *death* thing. In his mind, "Samantha Moon" died that night in Hillcrest Park, and something else jumped into her skin. I guess I can somewhat understand how he treated me the way he did these past few years since he no longer thought I was the woman he married, but some kind of impostor that only looked like her.

That still doesn't mean I forgive him. Okay, maybe I do a little since he's dead.

Naw, screw it. Still pissed.

Three cows, including the one oblivious to my having fed from her earlier, stick their noses close when I start crying over everything that happened with Danny. Geez. I brush my hand over the muzzle of the cow I drank from. "Go ahead and make me feel guilty why don't you?" It's like she senses my mood and wants to cheer me up.

I almost feel guilty for having fed on her. Well, at least I'm uniquely equipped to 'eat beef' without killing her.

I'm such a sap. Something, I knew, Elizabeth would have agreed on if she wasn't presently locked away in my mind.

Not long before sundown, a man and a boy emerge from the distant house and start heading my way. Well, not *my* way exactly. I'm sure they're interested in bringing their cows to a barn or something. I slip into the woods to avoid an awkward conversation. I don't expect they'd worry too much about a single woman trying to steal their livestock or doing anything unusual to them. But I also don't feel like dealing with the inevitable invitation to come inside and have dinner once the obligatory conversation happens around their inquiry at what I'm doing all alone out here.

Yes, I could influence them *not* to invite me. I could also influence them to forget they'd ever seen me. And I would, if I had to. But influencing means I have to dip into their minds. Dipping into minds isn't always a pleasant affair, trust me. I see things I can't unsee. Secrets that should remain secrets. Plus, it's getting old influencing, like, everyone I see lately.

Not to mention I don't even have the energy to

come up with a reasonable excuse this time. No, I'm feeling too close to getting home to think about anything besides getting that ring. And yeah, I know I'm "so close but so far away" and all. With my luck, Corporal Cokely is probably going to be dead, face down in the dirt somewhere I won't be able to recognize from the air. Maybe some medic or someone tasked with picking the dead is going to have taken that ring and I literally will spend the next hundred years trying to find it.

Ugh.

Once I walk a safe-enough distance into the forest so I can no longer see any sign of civilization in any direction, I remove my dress and bundle it together with my boots. Standing in the woods naked reminds me of being a kid again. We lived like hippies back then. Well, not so much me. I grew out of the whole nature girl thing around ten or eleven. Mary Lou never ran around bare-assed that I can recall. If she did, it happened before I was born, since she was six years older than me. My brothers on the other hand... especially Clayton. He *hated* clothes. The boy would lounge around the house all day in nothing but his skin, even if company came over. He even tried to go to school like that once, but fortunately, Mom and Dad put their feet down. Their bare feet, I might add. Honestly, I think they were more worried about a visit from CPS than anything else, but whatever. That was my childhood. It had been pure in a way I don't think society is even capable of anymore. We didn't have Nintendo games or smartphones. Just us and nature, and the occasional afternoon setting off fireworks.

I sigh down at myself. Undeath helped me get rid of a few extra 'mom pounds,' so my body is pretty damn close to how I looked in my younger twenties, although I still have natural curves. It's pretty frightening to think how dangerous a vampire could be if they fully gave in to their Dark Master. I start to wonder if that means the person they had been disappears entirely, or somehow still exists at that point, but stop myself. The last thing I need is to have Elizabeth trying to make bargains with me. At the very least, I might find myself in that very same pit I'd recently banished her into.

In the darkness of my closed eyes, I focus on the distant flame. It appears as a tiny pinpoint of orange light dancing deep within the void. At my behest, it draws closer, growing from a speck to a brilliant fluttering wisp of fire.

Talos emerges into the world on a wave of energy that makes me feel like I could wipe out the entire Confederate Army myself. I ride the charge into the skies after snatching up my clothes in one clawed foot, and steer generally northward. With the cover of the night above me, I climb high enough to see miles in every direction. Aside from the soft whisper of the wind and the leathery flutter of my wings, the world is silent.

From this altitude, it doesn't take me long to spot a large group of people in the distance. Much to my dismay, however, they don't look to be preparing to set up a camp but rather about to engage in a bit of night fighting. Great. Hopefully, the chaos will work in my favor.

I lean into my stride so to speak, flapping in great soaring down-strokes to gain speed. As best I can estimate, the group of Confederates is around twenty miles away give or take a few either way. They'd likely been walking since sunrise. That it's going to take me maybe ten to fifteen minutes to cover the same ground in the air makes me feel less wasteful for sitting around all day long. While I can't recognize any individuals this far away, or even *perceive* an individual apart from the mass of bodies, a small army does tend to stand out—especially when they're carrying a few lanterns.

That either means they're not expecting enemy contact or they're idiots.

However, the way they're forming up suggests they *are* preparing for a fight. The lanterns hover at the back of the ranks. I can't really tell who or what would be carrying lamps around at night during a battle, other than someone desperate to be shot. That could mean that the Confederates think they're up against a much smaller force and have zero chance of losing.

Or, maybe they're just morons.

As I draw nearer, dark shapes farther ahead become distinct from the terrain of grass and sparse trees. Due to distance, it still looks like I'm comparing two ant colonies rather than groups of people, but the Confederate side is easily five times that of the other group. I fly harder, adding a slight dive for additional speed. When I'm within a mile, they start trading shots. In the dark, the engagement happens at close range, between men taking cover behind trees, fallen logs, and whatever ditches they can find. Gunfire is far from rapid, so I suspect most of the soldiers are trying to hold as still as possible and wait for motion to shoot at. Sometimes, it's easy to forget how *dark* the 1862 night is to normal people. To me, it's dim, but I can still see easily for great distances. Were I mortal, I probably couldn't see a man five feet away.

This works to my advantage, as it lets me swoop in about fifty feet off the ground, circling over the Confederate position. My eyes are sharp enough to recognize faces from this height, so I keep gliding back and forth hunting for Cokely. As I drift closer to the Union soldiers they're clashing with, it becomes quite obvious why the gunfire is so sluggish: most of the Union guys aren't even armed.

Huh?

Curious, I head closer to them, and within a minute or two of looking them over, recognize at least three of the men I helped escape from the barn/jail days ago. Shit. This whole battle wouldn't be happening if I hadn't let them out. Battle… yeah, right. This is an execution. I gotta do something about this… but what?

Grumbling, I pull left into a hard turn, heading back for the Confederate side.

Within seconds of doing so, I happen to stare straight at Corporal Cokely. *Score!* He's about two-thirds the way to the right along their front line, at the edge of a thick patch of trees, down on one knee with his rifle aimed.

Perfect.

I dive at him. He looks up—likely hearing the leathery flutter—about half a second before I crash into him. Talos doesn't really have hands per se, but the bend along the leading edge of the wings kinda-sorta still works. My thumbs become stubby claw-like things that jut up from the bend. The leading edge from the bend to the tip is basically my index finger, with the smaller spars in the membrane equivalent to the rest of the fingers. In essence, I can think of these wings as enormous hands with membrane stretched between the digits.

Of course, they're shit for grasping and holding, but considering I'm crash-diving on top of him, it's enough to keep me riding him like a human bobsled as we slide through the underbrush. I release Talos back to his own world a few seconds before we come to a stop, yours truly perched rather nakedly atop a quite stunned Corporal Cokely.

He blinks up at me and his gaze shifts to my chest.

"Why, Corporal Cokely, I do declare!" I gasp in my best attempt to overact a startled Southern belle.

"I…"

Before he can yell or say much of anything, I

stare into his eyes and mesmerize him. Yes, just like Dracula from the movies, who, by the way, looked nothing like the real deal.

"Miss Moon," says a familiar voice from nearby. "Oh, my."

Startled, I look up as the ghost of George Clarke turns his back on me.

"You've nothing on!" says George.

"Side effect of switching forms," I mutter.

"Have you no shame?" he asks.

"I left my shame back in California," I say, and grab Cokely's right hand. My heart nearly explodes with joy at the sight of Delacroix's ring. "Finally! Some good luck."

"This skirmish should not be happening," yells George. "Those Yanks shouldn't be here."

"I know, I know," I say while wrenching the ring off a slightly-too-large-for-it finger. Come on, dammit. Don't make me have to take the finger off.

George risks a look at me for only a second before shying away.

"Good grief. Am I that horrible to look at?" I snap. "You're shying away like I'm Lilith herself or something."

"What are you doing to that man?" asks George.

"Taking this ring back. That's all."

Finally, it pops loose. I liberate a strip of fabric from his shirt and tie it through to make a pendant. The ring's a bit too large for a woman's finger and the last thing I'm about to do now is drop it. And it's definitely too small to fit over one of Talos' talons.

"Are you planning to just let this happen?" asks George, gesturing back at the intermittent popping of gunfire.

"Coke?" yells a man from behind me. "Corp'ral Cokely?!"

I'm momentarily tempted to nip a little blood from the corporal purely so I can claim to be drinking Coke during the Civil War. But, that whole Elizabeth getting more powerful thing stops me. Anyway, Cokely mumbles incoherently as my mental influence begins to weaken. His hand flops on my left thigh. He lifts his head, clearly surprised to feel a woman's skin, and slides his hand up to my hip like a blind person trying to confirm what their senses tell them.

"Sorry, Corporal." I lean down and stare into his eyes. "I have to insist you don't remember this."

Again, he gazes into nowhere.

At the hesitant approach of boots crunching twigs, I leap off the dazed man and shift back to my flying form. Wings spread, I crouch to leap into the air, but catch myself before I can leave the ground. Oops, I almost forgot my clothes. Now grasping my clothing and the pendant/ring in one taloned foot, I launch into the air not three seconds before a trio of Confederates stumble across Corporal Cokely.

"What in the Sam Hill?" asks one. "Coke, how'd you get back here?"

The corporal stares into the clouds.

"He dead?" asks the other, taking a knee. "Naw. Still breathin'."

Chuckling to myself, I swing around in a turn toward the larger mass of the Confederate Army. The view makes me think of one of Anthony's video games where he's got this spaceship thing and he's strafing bad guys on the ground with lasers. I daydream about orange energy bolts flying from my wing joints, blowing up Confederate soldiers—or at least blowing up the ground nearby and scaring them off.

Hmm. Maybe I *can* do something here.

The Union soldiers are mostly all still hunkered down since only like one in ten of them have weapons. I imagine they'd run if possible, but anyone who stands up is going to get shot dozens of times. So… they need a distraction.

Soldiers and sailors have one thing in common: superstition. If one man staggers back to camp with stories of some giant black dragon type thing, he'd probably get court-martialed (or whatever it is they do back in 1862) for being drunk on duty. If a whole unit sees the same bogey, it's more than likely going to become one of those things that they talk about only with each other until they die of old age.

That works.

I dive into the front line, rearing up and kicking one man in the face with my free leg. Well, not so much kicking as grabbing his entire head in my foot and flinging him over backward. The two men nearest him look at me… and I roar.

Before any bullets come my way, I power-flap straight up. Chaos spreads over the ranks like a drop of ink in water. I dash across their formation to the back and pounce on one of the lantern-bearers who turns out to be a maybe-thirteen-year-old boy holding the light for an officer to read a map. I catch myself at the last moment and simply push the kid to the ground rather than stomping him down. I also leave my foot on top of his face so he doesn't get a great look at me while roaring like hell at the officer —who promptly wets himself—and fly back into the air a second or two before a ripple of gunfire comes my way.

"Fools! Watch your fire," shouts the officer in a distinctly un-masculine tone of voice.

A low, swooping pass over their horses has the predictable effect of setting off somewhat of a stampede. With a loud *click*, a Minié ball bounces off my side. It hurts a little, kinda like a stiff punch, but Talos' scales laugh it off. Okay, this works. I can put up with a little pain especially since it doesn't seem like it will injure my extra-dimensional friend. Hell, if anyone in this battle deserves some pain, it's me, since it's my fault these men are here. Bleeding heart me just *had* to insist on saving Northerners. Some of those men are undoubtedly battle-wounded I brought back to the triage camp, who then wound up locked in the barn.

Well, here's hoping my playing fast and loose with history isn't going to have any lasting repercussions. So help me, if I get home and Jerry Springer is president...

I spend the next few minutes grabbing rifles away from soldiers and throwing guys around while roaring and shrieking like a literal monster. It's a bit busy around me to tell if the Union guys are taking the hint and getting their asses out of here. A couple more bullets bounce off my hide, but a few rip holes in my wing membrane. Ouch! That'll heal quick, but it's tender. Like seriously...ow! Imagine putting a staple through that delicate bit of skin between the thumb and index finger, and then make it hurt about twice that much.

Maybe I throw one or two soldiers hard enough to sprain a wrist or foot on landing, but I don't do any lasting damage.

One guy comes out of the crowd and rams his bayonet into my chest. Fortunately, he strikes a bony plate over my heart and I swear the tip of his bayonet bends. He looks at it, back to me, at it once more, and whimpers.

I lean toward him until our noses almost touch, and snarl.

The man flings his rifle off in a random direction and actually runs away, waving his hands over his head while screaming. It's like something straight out of a bad movie or a cartoon. I almost wind up laughing at the absurdity of it, but another Minié ball pings off the back of my skull hard enough that I see double for a second or two.

Grr.

I spin on the guy who shot me and roar. He, too, runs away, but doesn't drop his rifle.

Maybe six minutes after I'd decided to attack, all thousand or so Confederates are in full retreat. Wait, no. "Retreat" implies some semblance of order. They're scrambling in all directions with not the slightest bit of organization. Some even trample each other in their haste to get away. Soon, I'm standing alone in a field, wings folded across my chest in as arm-like a posture as they can manage, chuckling at my "victory."

A creature that shouldn't exist stopped a battle that shouldn't have happened.

Let's not talk about how that same creature had *caused* the battle in the first place, 'kay?

Still, it's kinda funny. I flash a toothy, dragon-like grin, imagining the stories these guys are going to be telling for years about what they saw tonight.

No one will ever believe them.

Chapter Twenty

Desperation powers my flight on the way back to the Pinkhams' farm.

As if my kids will be waiting for me in the room with Delacroix, I strain to fly as fast as possible—once I figure out which direction to go. The effort to find that ring has taken me quite a ways off, though despite that, I'm starting to recognize features of the land around here. That's not a good sign. I'm spending entirely too much time here. Focusing my every waking moment into trying to get home is the only thing keeping me from flipping out.

Well, every waking moment except for a couple times I had to sit around waiting for night, once by magical compulsion. Thanks to the very man I need now.

I close my eyes and let out a long, irritated sigh. As God is my witness, I will forgive Delacroix that humiliation if he helps me get back to my own time period. Honestly, I've been mesmerizing people left and right the past few days. Sure, it could be argued that I'm a hypocrite for being upset that he did the same back to me, but I'm a freakin' vampire. I'm *supposed* to do that stuff.

Thatsss more like it, Sssamantha.

Ugh. Great. If I'm doing something Elizabeth likes, that must mean it's evil. Guess she slithered out of my mental pit, like the true snake she is.

I've been called worse, and it's not evil, dear. It's your prerogative as a more advanced being.

Yeah…at least I'm not exploiting them or forcing them to do violent, dangerous things. I'll take some degree of comfort in that. Though, when it comes to protecting my family, a little mind reading to save time doesn't even approach anything that I'd feel guilty over.

By the time I reach the farm, it's less than an hour or so before sunrise. Grr. Damn delays. I risk landing right on their front porch—seeing Talos is nothing a little mental tweaking won't fix, okay, a lot of mental tweaking—and shift back into my human form. I hastily pull on the sundress before anyone spots me streaking around. No time for underthings or boots. I can put those on upstairs. I grab the knob and try the door, and it opens.

Wow. It really is different in the South. Even with a war on, they don't lock their doors. Well, I suppose it's a combination of the South plus 1862. I'm sure not every house down here in modern times leaves their door open, but I suspect many still do.

Silent as a mouse, I slip inside and shut the door behind me. I scurry upstairs carrying my bundle of footwear and unmentionables. The window at the end of the hall is already showing signs of blue and I barely make it into the guest room in time to stare at an empty bed before my body starts giving out under the press of dawn.

Frustrated, I try to yell, "Shit!" but it comes out as a barely-audible murmur after my cheek hits the floor.

***

The next thing I know, I'm in the bed that Delacroix had been resting on, staring at the ceiling. I'm not terribly big, but I doubt Lanie could've lifted me, so it had to be Burley Pinkham. My undergarments sit on the chair nearby, folded, the boots on the floor in front of it.

And, oh yeah, Delacroix is missing. Exactly as I thought he'd be.

"Dammit!" I pound both fists into the mattress on either side of my body.

Something hits the floor with a *thump* in a nearby room.

Lanie appears in the doorway a moment later clutching a bed linen to her chest, looking startled. "Miss Moon?"

"Yes. Sorry." I sit up, lift the blanket, and

swing my legs off the side. "I'm a little upset that Mr. Delacroix didn't wait for me to return."

She drops the sheet and shoots me a horrified stare.

For a second, I feel like I'm floating up and out of my body at an imminent sense of bad news. The last time I felt like this happened right before the doctor told me Anthony was going to die.

"Miss Moon," whispers Lanie, shaking her head. "Mr. Delacroix passed away in his sleep just the other night. Mr. Pinkham reckons he had been hurt awful bad inside like. I... I'm sorry."

I slump forward, head in my hands, staring at the floor between my feet. Dead? Delacroix is *dead*? He didn't flake out and leave me here, he had the gall to frickin' *die.* The reality that I'm more than likely stuck here for the next century and a half falls on me with the weight of finality. Image after image of my kids flicks across my thoughts, but no matter how much I want to hold them close, there's nothing I can do to make that happen.

Tears pat on the floorboards, first one, then two more, then I'm sobbing uncontrollably.

It's not fair. It's totally not fair. I only wanted to help Angela, why did fate throw me back here away from everyone I love and everything I know?

I'm dimly aware of Lanie picking up the sheet she dropped and backing away. Never before have I been so furious and so heartbroken at the same time. Weeping like I'd watched my kids die before my eyes, I can't even find the strength to fall over sideways on the bed. I'm stuck. I doubt I'll ever be able to convince Marie Laveau to help me, and I *still* have no real idea why that woman took such a strong dislike to me. Unless it's simple prejudice against vampires. Would Delacroix have any associates in New York who might be able to help? It's unlikely word of his death would reach there before me. If I could even find his home, maybe I could work out how to do something with that power source.

I mean, if a person who's clearly not immortal can learn how to do this stuff, I should be able to as well, right? It's not like I don't have the time to study. That would still be faster than waiting for the calendar to catch back up.

And what about Archibald Maximus? Where would he be at this time? Could I convince him to help me? Then zap his memory of our meeting? *Could* I zap his memory? He's a little more than a simple mortal after all. I sigh. I haven't a clue where in the world that man is, although I do know he's out there, somewhere.

I let out a long, pitiful sigh. Meanwhile, Elizabeth is unusually silent. Given this tremendous spike of sorrow, I really expected her to try the old sales pitch or something. Maybe the depth of my emotion is drowning her out.

"Miss Moon?" asks Lanie, closer than I expected.

I sniffle and wipe my face before looking up at the wide-eyed girl hovering beside me clutching

Delacroix's pack.

She sets the pack on the bed. "I think Mr. Delacroix knew he was dying, Miss Moon. He asked me to make sure you received this when you returned."

I look over at her again. Either I'm imagining things or she looks an awful lot like Tammy with light hair. Unable to help myself, I stand and embrace her like a proxy daughter. In my mind, I'm clinging to Tammy. I just need to hold my kids so bad... I...

"Miss Moon?" stammers Lanie. "Are you all right?"

I sigh. She's not Tammy.

"Sorry about that, I'm just a little emotional."

When I let go and take a step back, Lanie gives me this look that says "a *little?*" The poor girl's taken aback by my sudden show of emotion. "I'm really sorry for your loss. It's never easy to lose someone you care deeply about. Not a day goes by I don't think of my ma and pa."

"Oh." I wipe my face on my sleeve again and sniffle-chuckle. "We weren't close. I'd only met the man days ago. He was going to help with something extremely important to me."

Lanie bites her lip. "I see."

"Forgive me for that." I gesture at her. "You rather remind me of my daughter who's quite far away. I miss her, and my son, more than I can put into words."

"Dear me." Lanie gawks. "You've got a

daughter my age? How is that even possible?"

"I'm older than I look. Guess I've got good genes."

She tilts her head. "I'm sorry; I don't follow. Genes?"

"I mean, I suppose I got lucky. I'm in my thirties."

"In all my born days," she says, gasping. "Surely, you're pullin' my leg, Miss."

"It must be the healthy lifestyle." I smirk at my hands. "Sorry for coming unglued like that. Delacroix was going to help me get home and now, I'm not sure how I'll be able to see my family again."

Lanie glances at the door for a second, then back to me. "Oh, well, if you've nowhere to stay, I can talk to the Pinkhams. I'm sure they'd let you keep on here, at least a little while if not longer. We can always use some more help. The place is quite big, a bit too much for me alone to take care of. Missus Pinkham's always gettin' on Burley's ear about hirin' someone. She'd like to turn the place into an inn, I reckon."

Defeat sucks. If I've got no choice but to wait until the modern age returns, I suppose it won't hurt to spend a while around here and help out. Maybe I'll try to go to England and get on the Titanic so I can make damn sure they spot that iceberg. Or I could take Hitler out before he's anything significant. How hard could it be for me to manipulate my way in and kill him as a young soldier? Or even give him a mental command *not* to do the things he did. Which makes me wonder why didn't vampires already do that? Could he have been one? Or at the very least some other form of creature with a Dark Master inside? If so—and I shudder—he would be immortal and alive and well in modern times. Let's hope the bastard ate a bullet in his bunker.

Anyway, I could stop the JFK assassination or the start of the Vietnam War or any number of other things if my memory holds out and I don't get the dates wrong. But… surely there have been vampires all throughout history. Is there a reason beyond simple contempt for mortals that no vampire has ever interfered to stop such things? Of course, I have the perspective of having come from the future.

Then again, what if my memory of history is only the 'not really that bad' things that the vampires let continue? Could we potentially have been at the brink of nuclear war before and only by the mental influence of a vampire we avoided it? Would the Dark Masters welcome or fear the eradication of society? Nukes could put us back in medieval days, and I'm sure most of the extant vampires are rather fond of the finer things in life. Or maybe I have things backward. Maybe the vampires *caused* things like World War II at the behest of their dark masters. From what I saw at the battle of Manassas Junction, war is like an all-you-can-eat buffet for vampires.

"Miss Moon?" asks Lanie. "Are you feeling well? You slept so late, but it's almost time for lunch if you've a mind for it. Mr. Pinkham'll be in from the back field soon. Or I can bring you some soup."

I look up from the floor to her again. "I'm fine. My malaise is one of worry, not sickness. Lunch would be lovely, thank you. Please let me know when to be downstairs. I can help you set up for the meal as well if you like. Regarding your offer of talking to the Pinkhams about staying on here, I need a bit of time to think if that's all right."

"Of course, Miss." She smiles. "Good that you're well, then."

It might not be a bad idea to stay here at least long enough to settle my emotions. If I make any decisions now, they'd likely be rash and end in greater failure and disappointment. As much as I hate to think it, if Elizabeth is still concerned that I might actually succeed in stopping myself from becoming a vampire, I'm sure she'll do *something* to help.

Chapter Twenty-One

Sitting in silence for a while leaves my mind blank and my heart calm.

Elizabeth doesn't bother making herself known, though I can't even guess why. Maybe she thinks any possible interference would only push me deeper into a state of apathetic surrender and get me to pull this ring off at high noon and go up in flames. I'm not even close to that point yet. As long as there's at least a chance I could be reunited with my family again, I won't do anything that drastic.

Delacroix's pack stands out in its inconspicuousness beside me on the bed.

It's not quite a backpack, more a big leather satchel intended to be slung over one shoulder. To my eyes, it's something a hipster would probably carry, but I imagine they're somewhat common in this era, at least among people like Delacroix who wander frequently and don't have much to carry.

Curiosity gets the better of me, especially since the man had apparently left explicit instructions for Lanie to give it to me. I pull the flap open at the top, buckles clattering, and peer into a mostly-empty space about the size of an average modern kitchen trashcan. The sides, lined in deep crimson satin, have dozens of small buttoned pockets. At the bottom sits a leather-bound book with a scrap of red fabric sticking out the top.

Since it's the only thing in the bag, I take it out. The cover's plain and unlabeled, like one of those blank journals people sometimes keep. It's about two inches thick with a wad of silk stuck between the pages like a clumsy bookmark. Upon pulling it open at that point, I find a passage discussing something called a ley line. The handwritten text, which I assume is Delacroix's, describes natural conduits of magical power that crisscross the Earth. Places where they intersect are deemed 'nexuses,' and are rumored to contain vast amounts of magical energy. Somewhat akin to the planet being a living being with magic for blood, the ley lines would roughly equate to the circulatory system that carried it around. The more lines that intersect at a given point, the stronger the effect.

His notes detail cases of people becoming disoriented at these nexuses, of various phenomena like water flowing uphill or people experiencing hallucinations, even supposed sightings of mythical creatures and ghosts. A couple years ago, when I was still just normal old Samantha Moon, I would have likely thrown this over my shoulder and had a good laugh. However, after becoming a supposedly mythical creature myself, I'm not so inclined to merely chuck this aside like the insane drivel it appears to be. Especially not from someone who I *know* was an alchemist.

I shift the silk onto the left page and keep reading. Apparently, while he rested here waiting for me to return, he somehow managed to discern that a ley line nexus of five intersecting paths occupied a cave in the vicinity of Roanoke, Virginia, somewhat southwest of the city.

Hmm.

When I sit up straight to ponder this, the top end of the silk unfurls to let a small rock fall to the floor.

"A rock in silk…" I stoop forward and pick it up with two fingers. It's a common stone, no larger than an olive. "That's the analogy he used to describe me going back in time. Is he trying to tell me something?"

I flip the page. There, he writes that some cultures believed ley line nexuses act as portals or gateways to other times and places. Though, in his opinion, the intersection of so much magical energy didn't create a gateway in and of itself. He writes that they simply provided the power for the spells necessary to traverse time or distance that a practitioner could not draw out of thin air anywhere. In essence, he's thinking of these ley lines as giant power cables, only they're carrying magic instead of electrons.

"Why, my dear Mr. Delacroix… I do believe you're trying to tell me something."

I don't know why he didn't simply write *Sam, go to this cave and use the ring.* Or provide more detailed instructions like exactly *how* I'm supposed to use the ring. Did he think the "forces of evil" chased me around and might find this book before me? Or did he fear that Lanie or the Pinkhams might've read it and thought it the ramblings of a Satanist and burned it?

Hmm. Probably both.

I examine Delacroix's ring, which still hangs around my neck on a tattered cloth. It might fit on my thumb. I've been *using* two alchemist's rings more or less constantly for a while, but it's not like I needed to learn *how* to use them. Merely wearing them makes them work. Well, I suppose it wouldn't hurt to try.

After a brief shrug, I untie the cloth and jam my left thumb into the ring.

In seconds, my face, hands, and feet burst into flame.

"Yow!" I shout, yanking the ring off.

Okay, whoever said, "it won't hurt to try" has *clearly* never messed around with alchemy.

And, all right, I lied. I didn't shout 'yow.' I shouted something that rhymes with 'trucking hell,' likely the cause of Lanie dropping pots downstairs. Around here, it'd be shocking enough for a man to use such language. However, I stand by what I said.

A feeling like I just went bobbing for apples in a deep fryer warrants a bad word—or six.

I get a momentary peek at the bones inside the tops of my feet and my hands. Sizzling and snapping strands of muscles crawl back over them like some creepy alien worms. They thicken, growing back into muscle, then turn milky as new skin forms. By the time Lanie skids to a stop in the doorway, I look fine—though there's a noticeable haze of smoke hanging in the air.

"Miss Moon? What in tarnation happened? I thought I heard you say some right ungodly things." She sniffs. "Is that steak?"

"No. Mr. Delacroix has some rather *interesting* items in his pack. One of them caught me off guard and nearly lit me on fire. I shall endeavor not to open another until I'm nowhere near the house."

"Oh." She covers her mouth with one hand. "Are you burned?"

I show off my intact hands. "No. The smell is whatever substance he used to power the device. I'm honestly not entirely sure what it is."

She blinks, dazed. It's clear I lost her, which is fine. "You may as well come down once you dress. I'm starting on some sandwiches."

A tiny voice floats in the window, repeating "trucking hell." Only the little girl didn't exactly say that... she said what I said before.

Lanie damn near faints.

I give her a sheepish look. "Was that Ginny?"

She shakes her head, most of the color gone

from her cheeks. "No… Violet."

Great. I'm responsible for a five-year-old dropping the F-bomb. "I'll deal with it." I clap the book shut over the silk, stuff it in the pack, and head for the door.

"Miss Moon. Your boots?" She fans herself. "And mercy me. You've nothing on under that dress."

Shoes I could've skipped but, the luck I'm having… yeah. I rush back to get the rest of the way dressed, then hurry outside in time to distract Violet from saying *it* again and again. She's kneeling in a patch of wildflowers to the left side of the porch with a few dolls arranged around in front of her.

"Hello, Violet." I say. "Are you having fun?"

She looks up at me. "Yes, ma'am. My dollies are having tea in the grass. It's almost lunchtime, so we'll have to go inside."

"You heard someone say a bad word, didn't you?"

She nods eagerly. "Two of them."

"I know your mommy and daddy wouldn't want you to use those words."

"Well, someone yelled them. Why can't I?"

It was a good argument, admittedly, but one that would get her in a lot of trouble, which I just can't be responsible for.

It's time for a memory overwrite. A moment later, she's certain she heard "ducks and bells" which should save her from a childhood of whippings.

Smiling to myself, I head back inside to the kitchen where Lanie is busily cutting slices off a hunk of salted ham. "All taken care of," I say.

Lanie looks at me. "Taken care of?"

"Yes. I informed Miss Violet that she misheard me and was not pronouncing the words correctly when she attempted to shout 'ducks and bells.'"

Lanie giggles. "Oh, my. It's lucky her ma and pa didn't hear what she said before. Would've been heck to pay."

I grin. "Yeah, I can imagine. My son overheard my former husband using some words that no four year old should repeat once."

"Former husband?" Lanie's eyebrows start to climb with the suggestion of impropriety.

"He's deceased," I say, faking a sorrowful face. Well, mostly faking. I *did* mourn Danny, but that happened long before his heart stopped beating.

We assemble sandwiches and set the table.

Burley walks in from the back, swatting dust off his pants with his hat. "Ahh, our guest is awake. Are you feeling any better, ma'am?"

"Yes, thank you. I was simply exhausted when I returned last night." I fan myself. "Most kind of you to help me to bed."

He nods and takes his place at the head of the table. "My deepest regrets about that friend of yours. Doc said infection had set in. Bunch of, ehh...what'd he call it?" Burley looks around the dining room as if the walls would give him the word he's hunting for.

Susanna Pinkham glides in with the three girls in tow.

"Dear, what was it Doc Abernathy said 'bout that feller upstairs? Some sort o' raging?"

"Hemorrhage," mutters Susanna, clearly uncomfortable discussing such things around children.

Internal bleeding, which he could've survived in modern times. If I wasn't immortal, I'd be terrified to even breathe back in this time period. Over lunch, Burley grills me a little about who I am and what, if any, plans I've got. I tell him I'm from California, having traveled east after my husband passed away. I'd been heading to New York to look after an offer of employment, but it didn't pan out so now, I'm trying to get back to my children in California. Delacroix had been intending to help, but can't now for obvious reasons. Though I do tell them that he left me a note in the pack to check with an associate of his around Roanoke, which I plan to do soon.

And to placate Lanie, I mention that if it doesn't pan out, I'd be interested in maybe staying on here and helping out for a while. Lanie nods, smiling.

"What about your children?" asks Susanna. "Where are they now?"

"Still back in California, with my sister. I'm fixin' to get back to them as soon as I can, so I'm hoping Mr. Delacroix's associate works out."

The three of them nod.

"Ducks and bells," shouts Violet.

Susanna jumps and drops her sandwich. "What in tarnation?"

Her sisters giggle.

"That's my fault," I say. "I read the note and, well, it's something my daughter yells when she's happily surprised."

"Aww. I'm sure she misses you dearly," says Susanna, calming down.

I cross my fingers under the table. Hopefully, Tammy doesn't miss me at all—because, after all, she has no idea what's happened to me. No one does. "I'm sure. I should leave for Roanoke soonish."

"Heck of a trip," says Burley. "All the way 'cross Virginia. How you fixin' ta get there?"

"Oh, I'll manage." I smile and mentally nudge the conversation away from that topic. "This ham is quite good. Thank you so much again for your hospitality. I wish there was some way I could repay you."

Burley chuckles. "If you could go convince that Thom Chase to leave us the hell alone."

"Burl," mutters Susanna. "That's hardly something she need worry about."

"Oh, I ain't seriously thinkin' she'd do nothin' 'bout that fool."

I lean forward over the table to look at him. "Who's Thom Chase and why is he a problem?"

"Local busybody. Got wind of... well you know the help we provide to certain people in need. He might'a got wind of it. Least he thinks he did.

Tryin' ta stir up trouble."

"Oh. Where is he?" I ask innocently enough. "Maybe I can try talking to him."

Susanna shakes her head and waves me off. "None of your concern, missus."

Burley thinks about a scrawny, older guy who lives a mile or so down the dirt road that runs along the property's western limit. Thom Chase has that sort of squinty-eyed sour expression that really *does* make him look like the irritating nosy neighbor you really want to punch. "Yeah, I only said it in jest, missus. No sense you getting' anywhere involved with that man. He's got his demons."

"Yeah." I lean back in the chair thinking about how that man's demons could bring death down on the Pinkhams, and who knows what could happen to their three girls. 'Loyal' Southerners of this time didn't take too kindly to anyone caught helping slaves escape to the North, and enraged mobs aren't the most careful of things around children. "I know what that can be like. Demons, that is."

I get a raised eyebrow or two, but the family soon makes idle chitchat over the rest of the meal, and I'm happy to see that Lanie acts more like a daughter than a hired servant. I get the feeling that Burley is a man of few outward emotions, but he does care for all four kids in his care. Though, fifteen isn't really considered a child in 1862. My modern sentimentalities are showing.

After helping clean the plates and table, then sweeping the floor for crumbs (amazing how five-year-olds make the same-size messes in any era), I bid farewell to Lanie and head 'off to Roanoke.'

I do, however, pay a visit to Thom Chase before leaving the area.

He lives in a rather small green house on an overgrown lot a bit over a mile down the road. From the looks of the place, he hasn't put much care into things at all. If I were a kid, I'd think this is where the mean ol' man lived who keeps any baseball that lands in his backyard—and possibly drags any trick or treaters into his basement, never to be seen again.

Thom's reaction to my knocking is to shout, "Go away."

"Mr. Chase?" I ask. "I just need a moment of your time for a few questions."

Perhaps hearing a woman's voice catches him off guard. After a minute or two of silence, the rickety front door swings open to reveal a sixtyish guy with wispy hair and beard, deep-set eyes, and a hook nose. He shifts his jaw side to side, unsure what to make of me.

I peer into his thoughts. His confusion and irritation morphs into an urge to start complaining about my dress being too airy for a woman to be wearing out and about town. He thinks I've gone outside in a slip, or as he thinks of it, my underwear.

"What in tarnation are you doing, girl? Runnin' around out here like that. It's indecent."

Before he can launch into full-on rant mode, I steamroll over his brain. His posture slackens and he stares vacantly into space. No sense being seen here, so I guide him inside and plant him back in the cushioned chair he'd been in before, as evidenced by a little table with a tumbler of whiskey nearby.

The room stinks of tobacco and wet wood. I'm not entirely sure where that's coming from as nothing appears to be soaked. But hey, I'm not looking to buy the place, nor am I doing a random property inspection. Wow… I haven't thought of that in years. Speaking of which, I wonder what Chad Helling's up to now?

Well, okay, not *now*. He's not up to anything *now* since he doesn't exist yet. I mean around the time before that spell threw me back here. I haven't spoken to him in a long time, like at least six months. I should really call him when—if—I get home.

It takes a little longer than I expect to root around Chase's mind—the man is *damn* stubborn—but I erase his memories about the Pinkhams helping slaves escape. Or at least his suspicions. He thought he saw a 'pack of Negroes' creeping around the property at night, but never did find any tangible proof. He'd been ready to run to the nearest law as soon as he had something. Ugh. You know, as a former HUD agent, I used to like people who did that. But I can't help but want to bounce this guy's face off the wall a few times. What bothers me isn't that it's technically the law here or that the law is immoral, it's that this guy would take great glee in hurting those people.

While I'm in there, I leave a strong thought nugget about him owing Burley Pinkham $400 that he's hoping the man forgot about. That seems to be a good way to keep him from going snooping without causing the bastard any permanent harm.

Chapter Twenty-Two

Once again, I find myself wanting to fly and hesitating out of my fear of going up in broad daylight.

Damn nerve of people being freaked out by giant half-dragons, right? A girl ought to be able to get her shapeshift on any time of the day or night. So, instead, I wind up walking. I might not be going fast, but at least it lets me feel like I'm making progress. It also leaves me gazing around at the magnificence of nature in a time before freeways, billboards, jet planes, and so on. That I'm even able to appreciate this sight with the sun high in the sky reminds me how thin a line I'm really traveling here.

I mean, I'm a vampire walking across a grassy field in the middle of the damn day. There's no such thing as sunblock in this place. One little alchemist's trinket is keeping me alive right now.

Maybe it's reckless of me to risk being out in the wide open after all. I'm getting too casual about the whole sunlight deal, like I've almost forgotten how easily it can really kill me.

Which brings me back to Delacroix's ring. Why did putting it on cause me to spontaneously combust? Well, the ones I have on now constantly apply their "effect" to whoever wears them. That tells me that *his* ring has some "manner of effect" when worn, too. Still, I'm pretty sure that effect is *not* supposed to be lighting my ass on fire. Delacroix wore it just fine, no smoldering there.

He also mentioned its magic is in negation. Oh. That makes sense. I've got three magic effects active on me at once: tolerating sunlight, tolerating food, and being in 1862. Since only the time catapult required a human sacrifice to power, it's likely that wearing Delacroix's negation ring suppressed the effects of the other two, making me vulnerable to sunlight.

It also shielded him from my charm. Though, as best as I've come to understand my mental manipulation, they're not constant effects, more like a semi-permanent change. Think of magic like a hologram making an illusion. As long as the hologram exists, the thing appears there. Me playing with someone's memory is like digging a hole in the ground. If I stop digging, there's still a hole in the ground. But perhaps having the ring on prevented my proverbial shovel from scratching the surface.

Under most circumstances, I wouldn't really give much of a damn how this thing works, but since Delacroix had been inconsiderate enough to die, I've got to figure this out myself. I wonder if it could be as simple as just putting the ring on when I'm standing on this ley line nexus thing. At night, of course.

And that thought gets me panicking that the ley lines aren't going to do a damn thing.

But, hang on... Chloe said something about five paths. Seek the five paths and I'll find where I want to be or something.

Holy shit.

I stop walking, flop down, and pull open Delacroix's bag, grabbing the book and whipping it open to those ley line notes. My hands tremble from excitement as I scan over the shaky handwriting of a dying man. Roanoke has a nexus where *five* ley lines intersect.

Well, damn.

I stare into space and flip the book closed.

Five paths.

That woman told me the same thing Delacroix did, though I suspect I would've needed this ring. Or at least someone to teach me how to work a dispelling ritual. Well, that makes me feel somewhat better at not understanding the significance of what she told me days ago. I set the book back in the bag and, since I've got daylight to burn, decide to check out the pockets to see what else he might've had in here.

I pop open the buttons on the first one my gaze settles on. Inside a pocket barely big enough to hold a man's hand sits a scrap of lavender fabric. Snot rag or something I guess. I snatch it and pull, and wind up holding a friggin' top hat. The same one Delacroix had been wearing when I first saw him—which should in no way have fit inside that pocket.

After staring dubiously back and forth between said hat and said too-small pocket, I gingerly attempt to reinsert the hat where it came from. With a *schlurp* noise, the hat melts into a blur of pale purple and once again resembles a scrap of handkerchief tucked in a small, buttoned storage pouch.

"Well, shit. Don't see that every day."

I spend the next hour and change searching all twenty openings. He's got a few full suits, two pairs of nice shoes, undergarments, smoked fish, ink, quills, paper, several dozen esoteric books, and about $1,200 in paper money. The topmost pouch on the row closest to me holds a note written in the same shaky penmanship that detailed his research on ley lines.

"Dear Miss Moon," I read aloud. "I have come to realize I am soon to begin exploring the world after this one. I wanted to bequeath my travel pouch to you, though I will say a small part of me hopes you may, in turn, give it to either another alchemist or one who walks in the Light." I nibble on my lip, thinking of Anthony. "To someone whose mind has not been opened to greater possibilities than the humdrum, they will see twenty plain pockets too terribly small to be of much use. Those who know that greater things exist will see this bag as it truly is. I wish you luck in returning home. Regards, Jean Delacroix."

Well, this will come in handy. And no wonder Pardoe and Chisholm left the bag behind... they saw twenty tiny pockets with nothing but lint in them.

And no wonder Delacroix's spirit didn't hang around, either.

He was off exploring new worlds.

***

Once it gets dark, I again strip to my birthday suit. Only this time, I pack my stuff in the bag, not bothering to use any of the magical pouches as the normal interior has plenty of room.

Out of curiosity, I again try putting Delacroix's ring on my thumb. This time, I don't ignite. So, yeah. Wearing that ring cancels the effect of any other magic working on me. At least magic that didn't require a vast amount of power to invoke. For now, I leave it dangling on the scrap around my neck and call Talos across worlds. Sometimes, I wonder what he does with my body while I'm borrowing his. It's not like humans really have much to offer a dragon. We can't fly. We're not particularly strong or tough. I can't imagine we even look all that attractive to reptiles, except maybe as a snack.

I snag the pack in my talon and flap as straight vertical as possible, heading up about two hundred or so feet off the ground into the concealment of a newly dark sky. There's still a haze of reddish-orange across the western horizon, which comes in rather handy as a navigation aid. Richmond is still in sight behind me and a little off to the north. As I understand, Roanoke is almost due west of it about 160 or so miles. Since I don't have a smartphone or integrated GPS, I'll have to trust my senses to keep me going in as straight a line as possible.

My need to get home as fast as possible conflicts with my need to get home at all. I don't want to zip around in circles all damn night, so I fly at a brisk but not reckless speed, keeping a decent amount of attention on the ground to track landmarks. Way off to my right, the cook fires of a military camp dot the landscape. Some part of me feels guilty that I'm not doing more to stop this conflict; then again, I shouldn't be here at all. It's so bizarre to see the land below me in an age before electricity. Everything is *so* dark, and it makes the stars seem brighter. The air smells much fresher (except when I fly over farms and get a nose full of cow crap). It's almost tragic what we've done to the planet in a century and a half. But, yeah, that whole modern medicine thing—that's hard to give up.

After about two hours of silent flight, I spot a large-ish city and head for it.

From the air, it's reasonably easy to find an

area of hills a few miles southwest from the city that look promising to house caves. Of course, I'm not expecting to see giant glowing blue lines on the ground. If they worked that way, I'd surely have encountered a ley line or two back home. Assuming, of course, vampires can see them. I can't imagine they're much different than ghosts, but... since I've never *seen* a ley line and I *have* seen ghosts...

I do, however, catch a flicker of blue light. It's not a line, though, it appears to be George Clarke jumping up and down while waving at me. He recoils as I dive in close, having a fairly typical reaction for a sixteen-year-old boy to the sight of Talos. Since I don't immediately want to cry over his death again, I think I might have found peace with his fate. After all, I know for a fact there's a cycle now. My son "learned everything he needed to learn" far too young and was ready to go back into the mixer so to speak. Only, I wasn't having it. I didn't really understand the cycle then, and even if I did, I still would've done the same thing.

No one, not even God, is going to take my son away from me. At least, not when he's only a little boy. Sure, being immortal, I know I'm going to be there to watch my children die at some point— hopefully when they're both elderly. It's going to be the hardest thing I've ever done or will do, but knowing they've had a full life might let me keep going. Maybe once that day comes, I'll search the world looking for their reincarnated souls. Or would that be fair to Tammy and Anthony? And to their new mother? Me, a relic from a previous life forcing myself into their new existence for my own desires.

Ugh. I don't need to think about this now. I need to get home to them.

George forces himself to look at me as I land in front of him. "Miss Moon, that is a truly frightening aspect of your personality."

I shrug, flapping an arm at my face in hopes he understands I can't speak in this form.

"I know what you are looking for here, and it is close. We can walk if you fancy."

Great. I close my eyes and offer my thanks to Talos for his kindness in helping me once again. The sense of him bowing his head in acknowledgment comes back, and soon, the warm Virginia wind brushes across my bare chest.

"As long as I live I will never… well, I suppose that's out the window. The living part, that is." George smiles. "Still, never am goin' ta get used to a woman so brazen while I live *or* die."

I squat over the pack and open it. "It's only brazen when it's done for no reason other than showing off. I'd rather not ruin the only things I have to wear. If a lady found herself in the bath when the house caught fire, would she stand around dressing or get out?"

George averts his eyes as I pull on my clothes. "Depends on the lady, Miss Moon. I've met a few who'd rather burn first." He chuckles.

"What, there's a lady present?" I feign looking around.

He snickers, opens his mouth, and shuts it without comment, an awkward expression on his face.

"You were going to say you'd seen a few you'd hope would choose to burn, since some people are better off never being seen *au naturel*. I get it."

"*Au naturel*?"

"Naked."

If ghosts could blush, I'm sure he'd be beet red. As it is, he looks away. "I don't engage in such talk, ma'am."

I laugh. "Look, I spent years working around cops and federal agents. I'm no stranger to 'locker room talk.'"

"Beg your pardon, ma'am. Locker room?"

I chuckle while shaking out the dress so it falls around my legs. "Something from the future, forget I said that."

George turns to look at me again once I'm 'decent.' "I am afraid these strange things you speak of are unknown to me."

"You'll find out eventually. Two, maybe three, maybe four lives from now. So, which way should we go?"

George nods off to the left, then starts walking. "More lives?"

"I've come to learn that souls keep going around and around. Mine came from a long line of witches, believe it or not."

He looks me up and down. "That doesn't shock me, ma'am."

Again, I laugh. While following my ghostly friend through the foothills, I explain how he's likely to be reborn, live a life, die again, be reborn, and so on, until his soul has learned whatever lessons it's fated to learn before merging once more with the Creator.

"What about you, Miss Moon? How long are you going to live as a vampire?"

"Until the end, I'm afraid. I got kicked off the merry-go-round, so to speak."

"Oh, I'm sorry."

"It really is hard to mourn past lives I don't remember and future lives who won't remember me. Or wouldn't have remembered me, since they won't happen now. And when I cease to be, no trace of me will be around to feel sad about that. Or even realize I no longer exist. Nothing worth getting maudlin about while I'm still here."

"You sound a lot like my father," says George. "He says stuff like that all the time. Like 'the dang thing already broke, gettin' riled up over won't do a dang thing.'"

"He sounds like a wise man. Even with all the dangs."

I wink and George grins.

A few minutes later, my ghostly guide points at a cave mouth and heads inside. I follow. The tunnel winds back and forth for a couple hundred feet. The unusual roundness of the walls suggests it may have carried water at one time.

"Pa thought I was foolish for joining up to fight. I reckon he was right. But not because I wound up dead."

I tilt my head. "No?"

"Naw. Now I see it's just a whole bunch o' boys like me. Poor and little ta their name all fightin' o'er what a handful of wealthy landholders wanna do."

"Sorry, George. I hate to say it, but the same crap is still happening where I'm from. Only it gets worse as the weapons get bigger and crueler." The deeper I go in the cave, the stronger a sense builds of an electric-like charge in the air. "I can feel something," I say. "Energy."

"You see 'em now, don't ya?" asks George.

It occurs to me that he looks almost solid, but still luminous. "No. But you're brighter. More real looking."

George glances down at himself. "Huh, fancy that. I can see this light on the ground, under yer feet. Like we're both walkin' on a road made out of the moon."

"Heh. Moon walking on the moon. Kind of ironic. No, I don't see any light except for you."

"Well, come on this way then. Looks like a bunch of 'em cross up there in that yonder chamber."

"Five?" I ask.

"You can see 'em?"

I shake my head. "No, but I was told to find the

place where five of them intersected."

"Inter-what-ed?"

"Umm. Crossed."

"Oh. Why dun' ya just say 'crossed' then?" George blinks at me.

"Sorry."

"Fancy future word, huh?"

"Something like that."

George leads me into a spot that couldn't have been much more obvious to what I'm looking for. Five similar cave tunnels, all smoothed by the passage of ancient water, continue out from the walls of a chamber about thirty feet across. Though I can't see any visual sign of ley lines, it's easy to picture them extending out from these caves to intersect right in the middle of this dome-shaped room. I wonder if these ley lines guided the ancient rivers that formed this catacomb, or if the water came first and concentrated the magical energy to make the ley lines.

"Well, this is the place," says George. "How's it fixin' ta get you back where ya need ta be?"

"That's the part I still need to figure out."

I kneel at the point where the lines I've imagined all come together. While I still can't see anything, there *is* such a potent charge in the air that I feel like I've chugged six *pots* of coffee and have both hands on a Van de Graaff machine.

"Miss Moon. That ring." George points.

"Which?" I peer down at my hands, but it's not them... Delacroix's ring is glowing blue. "Wow.

Never saw anything like this before."

"It's pretty like…." He smiles. "Well, like you."

"Aww, George. I'm old enough to be your mother."

He stares. "Naw, shucks. I can't believe that."

"Right, so…" I pull Delacroix's journal out, but it doesn't say anything about a ritual or how to 'activate' the ring. "Maybe it is as simple as putting it on."

George shrugs.

"Well, George. Thank you for all your help. If this works, I might not have the time to say anything more, so I'm doing it now. Whatever happens for you in the future, I hope your next life makes up for this one getting cut short."

He tips his cap at me. "You did a wounded boy a great kindness. If there's any justice in this world, I'll 'member ya. If'n what you said's true an' all about goin' 'round in circles, God willin' I have any daughters, may I 'member you enough ta name one Samantha."

"That's so sweet." I reach out to take his hand, but get only a grip of static electricity prickles. "I'm sorry I couldn't do any more to save your life here."

"Well, you said we all learn what we need to learn then go back for the next round. Guess I dun figgered it out, but I wish I knew what 'it' was."

I chuckle. "Don't we all. Well. Farewell, George. I need to go home. Thank you again for all your help."

He nods.

I hold a breath, wish like hell to go home, and jam my thumb into the negation ring.

…and nothing happens.

"Is it workin'?" asks George.

"No."

You need to activate the ring, Sssamantha, whispers Elizabeth. *The magic imbued in it has both passive and active effectsss.*

"Great. So how do I activate it?" I ask.

"No idea, ma'am," says George.

"I'm talking to my inner… umm… visitor," I mutter.

It is a sssmall incantation. I would be pleasssed to recccite it for you. A little control, enough to speak.

"Or I could just wait 150 years and stop myself from going out jogging that night. Do you want to roll those dice?"

A reptilian sigh slides across the back of my mind. *Clutch the ring in your right hand. Hold it out in front of you over the nexus.*

That sounds harmless enough, so I do.

Focusss your will into the ring that it worksss, and chant: Alba wabatu sawf taftah. Saharun sawf yakun.

She repeats the words again, slower, over-pronouncing them.

For some reason, I think this is going to work. I sling the bag over my shoulder, nod once at George, and hold the ring out once more.

"Alba wabatu sawf taftah. Saharun sawf yakun."

A flash of white energy blasts off the ring and hits me in the chest with a near-deafening roar and electrical buzz. It feels as if my body plunges into a swimming pool full of energy. Seconds after the flash, a force that's soft and crushing at the same time slams into me from in front, like I got hit by a nerf bus. I spin head over ass-backward and start to fall…

Chapter Twenty-Three

With a tremendous *whump*, the brilliant glare fades, leaving me seeing only darkness.

The silence soon gives way to a throng of chanting. Cold wind flutters the dress between my shins and whips my hair to the side. For a second that feels like a minute, I hang in midair directly over the voodoo ritual that shot me back in time. I'm once again over Bayou St. John, staring down at Angela Jenkins, her pale, naked body laid out on a sacrificial altar. Hundreds of cultists, every last one of them nude, surround us, chanting to their god Zonbi…or something like that. Another pair of men beat out a rhythm on large drums.

Near the altar in an enormous cage, an immense serpent sways side to side, its gaze locked on Angela as she cries out, "Papa, take me! Papa!"

Marie Laveau is the only one here (other than me) wearing anything at all, a simple white shift and gold bangles on her wrists and ankles.

I've appeared a few seconds *before* I left. A shadow moves above me—Talos, rather prior-*me* swooping in, exactly as I did before I was sent into the past.

Helpless to do anything but fall, I drop some twenty-odd feet and land flat on my chest in a smallish clearing between the ring of cultists and the altar. *Oof.* At least the grass is soft... and my bones are a little tougher than a mortal's. Being flat on the ground is not a great tactical position, so I spring upright.

"*Canga bafie te!*" Marie Laveau shrieks at me, waving the knife like a wand. "*Bomba hen hen!* You not welcome here, creature of the night! Go, before Papa Limba come to take you away with him!"

"No!" shouts Talos-me from the air.

Marie Laveau looks upward, bewildered.

Talos-me flies down closer, slashing at the voodoo queen. Great flapping wings beat up a storm, making the nearest cultists flinch. Lightning cracks the sky, and the crowd around us—most of them fallen into a trancelike state—snap out of their haze, becoming aware of my presence. The dancers on either side of Laveau howl and reach up as if to grab Talos-me and drag it/her to the ground.

A loud clap of thunder seems to galvanize the crowd, and the big drum starts up again.

Queen Marie, still sparring with Talos-me, chants, "Papa Limba! Papa Limba! *Envoyer*—"

Oh hell no. Not again! I dive across Angela and punch the bitch square in the nose.

The instant my knuckles make contact, Talos-me disappears.

Angela's eyes flick open all of a sudden, wide as Moon Pies as she screams, "Papa take me! Pa-paaa!"

Marie Laveau charges back and shoves me aside with surprising strength, sending me sliding over the wet grass on my back, my legs in the air. While Angela keeps begging for her papa, Laveau raises the blade over her. Angela, amazingly, grins like she cannot wait to die.

"No!" I shout. I'm surrounded on all sides by her devotees and have a mere second to react, so I do the only thing that comes to mind: I teleport on top of Angela.

The knife rams down into my back, deflecting off my spine and going all the way through me. It probably still pierces an inch or so into Angela, but the wound isn't fatal. The young woman under me wails in ecstasy at the pain.

Before Marie Laveau can process what just happened, I clamp on to Angela, call the single flame, and teleport the pair of us onto a lower branch of one of the giant trees directly in front of me, a couple hundred feet away. We're far enough away that the cultists should have no damn idea where we went. And, as far as I can tell, I hadn't teleported us into a wayward branch, which would have hurt like hell.

"Papa, no!" shouts Angela, struggling to get away from me.

Shit. If she keeps shouting, they'll find us. I clamp a hand over her mouth. Grr. It's kinda difficult holding on to a naked, bloody young woman revved up on something that makes her stronger than she ought to be. This girl has got to be possessed. How am I going to—

Wait…

I grab her hand and transfer Delacroix's ring onto her thumb. The instant it's on her, the milky glaze in her eyes disappears and she stares at me with an expression of complete confusion. Once I'm sure that whatever charm had been affecting her is gone, I pull the ring off her.

An inhuman screaming roar rises up from the middle of the ring of cultists. It's not coming from Marie Laveau, but from the very air in front of her. She stares in horror at the empty altar and the bloody knife. Ooh, I can only imagine her voodoo god Zonbi or whatever is *not* happy with vampire blood on his altar—or the tease of a stolen sacrifice.

Angela clings to me, shivering at the cold night air on her naked body. We both stare in horror as a roiling mass of black energy wells up from the altar. The vapor plumes twist together into a serpentine coil that lashes out at the priestess like a cobra strike, blasting all the flesh from her skeleton that remains upright, twitching. Sweet mama. The priestess' eyeballs, still in the sockets of a skull coated only in blood, pivot up to stare at the out-of-control magic.

Marie Laveau's bones begin to collapse backward; the jawbone opens, but no scream comes forth.

Cultists wail and scatter in all directions as the mass of volatile black energy engulfs the toppling skeleton in a column of shadow. In seconds, the malevolent energy seeps back into the altar, leaving no trace the priestess had ever existed. A wail of sirens rises in the distance. Eulalie's made good on her promise to send the police in after us. I *knew* they wouldn't get here in time.

"Oh, shit," whispers Angela. "What the fuck did I just watch? Ow. Damn, I'm stabbed. What happened? Why the hell are we up in a tree… and what happened to my clothes?"

I grasp her head in both hands and stare deep into her eyes. She doesn't need to remember the being so close to death *or* getting involved with Eulalie's crew of vampires. She'd been jealous of Wendy, and overly affected by their feeding on her. According to Eulalie, she'd been unsatisfied merely being a thrall and demanded they make her into a vampire, too… so they'd banished her. I do my best to make her forget vampires exist. "You were abducted by a group of weirdos."

She blinks a few times. While she's lost to the mental fog of her brain trying to process my new information and deal with the forced removal of the last few minutes, I teleport us to the ground and try to get my bearings.

Once I figure out which way to go to find Eulalie and her SUV, I pick Angela up and carry her across the muddy ground. It's still hot and steamy, and every step releases a stink like raw sewage from the muck. At least I have boots… and my sundress.

Angela squirms and tries to get away.

"Hey…" I hold her tight. "You're okay now. I got you. Keep pressure on that wound, okay?"

"Who stabbed me?" She stares at the blood all over us both.

"A woman."

"Did she get you, too?"

Her showing no reaction to being stark naked is making *me* feel embarrassed. "One of the nutjobs did. Everything was moving so fast I didn't get a good look at her. She came rather close to nicking me as well, but what's all over me is your blood," I say, cringing inside at the blatant lie. Of course, the hole that knife left in me is already gone.

"W-who are you?" Angela, shivering in fear, scans my face. We are, after all, only inches apart.

"I'm a private investigator, hired by Wendy's parents. Heard you were missing, too, so I decided to come looking for you."

She blinks. "I don't remember how I got here. What happened to me?"

I pat her shoulder. "I'm sorry. I can't answer any of that. I tracked you to this park and those nuts were about to hurt you, so I charged right in. Not my best plan. They scattered and took off… except for that one bitch with the knife."

"Where'd she go?" Angela looks around at the creepy trees.

"Not sure. Too much chaos. Don't worry about her. We need to get you to a hospital."

Angela looks down at herself. "All my shit's gone. Like why am I naked?"

"Creepy cultist sacrificial ritual 101," I say. "The victim and all participants must be naked."

She stares at me. "What?"

"That group that wanted to kill you gave you something. You were so high you had no idea what you were participating in."

She shivers. "Holy shit. Why don't I remember... like the past week?"

"Someone drugged you—with what, I don't know—and abducted you. Whatever they gave you must have affected your memory. You're okay now, Angela."

"Oh. Ow, this hurts like a lot."

I glance down at her, half-tempted to make a remark about the priestess' knife having gone completely through me... with this girl only getting an inch or so. But, honestly, what was the point? "Yeah. Stab wounds usually do. Keep pressure on it."

Well, I suppose going back through time had one little advantage: I've got a beat-to-hell sundress on. If my initial plan had worked—swooping in there as Talos and snatching her like an eagle nabbing a field mouse—neither one of us would be wearing anything. It's awkward enough that she's nude, but *both* of us...I think I'd develop a permanent blush.

Eulalie leaps out of her SUV when we get within sight. Moon Bayou behind us is awash with police lights and shouting, cops running around chasing naked cultists. Boy, I wonder what that's going to look like on the news tomorrow.

"*Mon dieu!*" shouts Eulalie. "What has happened?"

I carry Angela over to the back passenger door on the right. "Remember when I said this was probably the dumbest plan I ever had?"

Eulalie blinks at me. "And I told you not to do it? I remember."

"Yeah, well... it *was* a pretty damn stupid plan. But I've had a lot of time to think about it."

"What?" Eulalie tilts her head. "You are making no sense."

I set Angela on the seat and mutter, "Keep your hands pressed over that wound."

"Samantha," says Eulalie. "What..."

"I'll explain." I climb in and shut the door. "Thanks for waiting, by the way."

She runs around the front and pulls herself into the driver's seat, then glares at me.

"Now everything makes sense," I say. "How people knew me, but I couldn't remember..."

"Samantha, did something happen to you?" asks Eulalie.

"Yeah. I'll explain later, once we get Angela to

the hospital." I glance over at her. "I just got back from Richmond."

She starts the truck and blinks at me. "Richmond? How…you were only gone a few minutes."

"Like I said, we'll talk."

Chapter Twenty-Four

Eulalie drops me off back at my hotel after we'd scrounged up some clothes for Angela.

Bringing a naked, wounded young woman to a hospital might connect her back to that nonsense in the bayou, so we all decided on a simple mugging story for the authorities. Mostly to keep Angela separated from the voodoo mess.

I also made damn sure she knows she should probably get the hell out of Louisiana as fast as possible. *Something* horrible happened to Marie Laveau, but that doesn't mean the other hundred or so of her followers won't remember Angela. So, she agreed to get out of here. Then again, there was a small chance I might have prompted her to agree.

So, anyway. It's true that the driving force behind my everything in the past couple of weeks has been getting the hell back to my kids, but now that I'm free of the tremendous weight of wondering *if* I will ever get home, there's something I *really* want to do first.

I peel off the bloody, ancient sundress, kick off my boots, and sashay into the hotel bathroom.

"Come to mama, you hot piece of total sexiness," I say—to the shower stall.

***

After a nice long shower, I enjoy a nicer *longer* soak in a bath. It feels like I'm washing the grime of a thousand years away. All the dirt under my pointed nails, the grit that seems to have found every little crevice of my skin. When I first turned on the water, I thought a spray tan rinsed off me, but it had been *dirt.*

Once I'm clean, dressed, and packed, I head down to the front desk to check out. And, after a nice little walk to an inconspicuous place outside, I teleport home to an always-empty section of my closet, there just for such an occasion. With Delacroix's ring and his magic travel bag stashed safely in my bedroom safe, I rush down the hall.

Tammy's on the couch in the living room watching TV. "Oh, hey, Mom."

She looks back to the screen for a second or two, then snaps her head to stare at me. "Mom! Where'd you…?" Her confusion melts away when she remembers I can teleport. "Oh. Cool. So you're done in Louisiana?"

I rush over and pounce-hug her.

"Gah! Mom! Chill out. You're acting like you've been gone for months." Tammy blinks and reads my mind. "Whoa, you went to a Civil War thing?"

Anthony leans in from the kitchen, peanut butter on his cheeks. "Oh, hey, Mom."

"Get over here," I say, sniffling and raising my arm.

"Mom's on Planet Weird again," says Tammy.

As soon as my son sits on my other side, I squeeze both of my children tight, too choked up to talk. Anthony looks so much like those boys who ran headlong to their deaths in Manassas. To think that mere children fought and died in such a horrific conflict gets me all sorts of clingy. And Tammy does kinda resemble Lanie, in that they're both teenage girls with pale skin. Their faces aren't really *that* similar after all. Guess I'd been projecting.

Tammy gasps at the same instant I relive the emotions of realizing I almost watched a fifteen-year-old get shot in the face, if not for my offering to clean dishes. "Holy crap, Mom. You *really* went to the Civil War?"

Elation at having my kids close and safe pulls me out from under the cloud of sorrow. I poke her in the side. "Young lady, we've talked about mind reading in the house."

She's too stunned at what she's seen in my head to even turn on her sarcasm machine.

"Say, um, who won the Civil War?" I ask.

"The Blue Team, duh," said Anthony.

I breathe a sigh of relief. "The North?"

"Of course the North. And whoa," says Anthony. "You legit went back in time or something?"

I pull them both in tight. "It's…a long story."

They exchange glances.

"A *real* long story," I say, then laugh.

The End

About the Authors:

J.R. Rain is the international bestselling author of over seventy novels, including his popular Samantha Moon and Jim Knighthorse series. His books are published in five languages in twelve countries, and he has sold more than 3 million copies worldwide. Please find him at: www.jrrain.com.

Originally from South Amboy NJ, **Matthew S. Cox** has been creating science fiction and fantasy worlds for most of his reasoning life. Since 1996, he has developed the "Divergent Fates" world, in which Division Zero, Virtual Immortality, The Awakened Series, The Harmony Paradox, and the Daughter of Mars series take place.

Matthew is an avid gamer, a recovered WoW addict, Gamemaster for two custom systems, and a fan of anime, British humour, and intellectual science fiction that questions the nature of reality, life, and what happens after it. He is also fond of cats. Please visit him at: www.matthewcoxbooks.com.

Made in the USA
Columbia, SC
29 June 2019